McCauley's Rest

Barry Joyce

This is entirely a work of fiction. No person, place or organisation bears anything but a tenuous relationship with reality.

Copyright © 2014 B V Joyce

All rights reserved. This book or any part thereof may not be reproduced in any form without the author's previous consent.

Chapter 1

The Desk Sergeant led Harry out of the station onto the forecourt where a yellow cab was already waiting. Sergeant Hammer was a bull of a man, with a ruddy face that readily cracked open in a wide toothy grin as he yanked open one of the rear doors.

"I ain't sure who you are, Mister, but you done us a big favour. We're mighty grateful, and that's for damn sure"

Harry smiled, nodded briefly, and handed him his stick to hold while he eased himself into the back seat and stretched out his long legs.

"He'll take you to the airport right now," said the Sergeant as he slammed the door shut. Briefly, he leant through the front window to speak to the driver then turned, raising a farewell hand as he started back into the station.

Even after his stay in hospital, Harry was still feeling exhausted from all his recent exertions and was happy to lie back and let the journey just happen. The nightmare was finally over. He was going home.

Warm images of Tatyana welcoming him through the front door drifted across his mind as he idly watched the city passing by the cab window. He was so happy to be leaving behind the bustle, the noise and the gaudy neon that competed for attention with the Las Vegas sun, even in mid-afternoon.

Eventually, the downtown cityscape gave way to houses and shopping malls, until they were finally on the open highway with only an occasional building peppering the desert sands.

Suddenly Harry was wide awake, and he shot upright in the seat. This was not right. McCarran is a city airport. Surely there was no desert between the city and the airport – not the airport he knew. He leaned forward and tapped on the glass screen. The driver turned his head and smiled. Harry's stomach lurched as he recognised the man under his old-fashioned flat cap. He was one of Fossen's men who had held him in his hotel room.

Harry hammered at the screen but soon realised it was made of armoured glass. The driver smiled once more as he frantically flipped the door locks, but they had been immobilised. He was trapped - a prisoner in a yellow cab. He knew then that the Mob was to have the last say, and he was being taken for that final ride after all. And it took no time at all to guess where they were headed.

Within ten minutes his fears were confirmed as the cab turned off onto the dirt track that he knew led to McCauley's Rest.

Chapter 2

Only occasionally would the more intrepid tourist step off into the Calle Siracusa, his camera bobbing on his chest as he negotiated the shallow cobbled steps leading down towards the old harbour. He would be seeking that definitive shot of old Naples that his friends and relatives were waiting so patiently to see on his return.

Little colour decorated this ancient street. The sun only ventured between the high walls for one short hour each day to bleach the shadows. At all other times, it was a grim scene, illuminated only by many shades of grey.

At about a hundred yards, a strange frisson in the hairs at the back of his neck would cause the intruder to halt abruptly. His pulse and heart beat would move up a click or two. Suddenly, he would be aware of a hundred pairs of eyes staring at him from behind the blind windows, urging him further into their owners' trap. The braver souls might snap a quick photo, but all would saunter as nonchalantly, but as rapidly, as possible back up to the sun-washed sanctuary of the Via Toledo.

Harry swept past this point with no such fears. He had been here once before and besides, he was here by invitation. He was somewhat late and hurrying in an attempt to make up time. Any natural grace of movement he possessed was thwarted by the shallow steps, which were more than one full stride deep, resulting in a rather inelegant lope.

Some fifty yards further on, he turned off to the right into an even narrower alleyway. Here, the houses on either side seemed to reach out to meet each other, making it darker still. Harry was guided towards a light, visible even nearing midday, at the end of the alley which opened out and was then terminated by a large house. This had once been the pride of some rich merchant, but was now decrepit from many decades of neglect. The main door was open and Harry followed the light.

As he entered the room, clearly used as some unnamed and unheralded bar for locals, he immediately saw that nothing in it had changed since his last visit several years earlier. The same gaunt barman leaned across the small bar that had been roughly formed in a doorway to the right. As Harry approached, he unfurled his body from the counter and invited an order with the very slightest twitch of his head.

"Cold beer, please," said Harry.

Using both hands simultaneously the barman reached up to unhook a glass and into a fridge for the beer, placing them both down on the counter. Harry's hand went into his pocket for some change, but a slight shake of the head followed by a nod in the direction of the far side of the room announced that the drink was already paid for.

Harry took a swig straight from the bottle and turned to survey the dingy room. It was lit by half a dozen bulbs hanging from the high ceiling by their original brown fabric flex, dangerously threadbare in places. Only half of them were still topped by their green metal shades. Whatever colour the walls were last painted, they were now a dark shade of brown, only slightly lighter than the ceiling which had taken the brunt of the layers of tobacco smoke over the years. The paint on all the woodwork was crazed and blistered.

There were half a dozen or so tables, all now empty save one at the far end, alongside a small raised dais which Harry presumed was probably the focus of the occasional dubious form of entertainment. Four men sat at the table but, as he watched, one of them got up and left the room. A moment later, a slight weasel of a man got up and, sidled past him without a glance, eased a newspaper out of his pocket and settled himself to read at a small table by the entrance door. Taking this activity as his cue to join the party, he moved over to the far table.

The man sitting opposite Harry as he approached simply stared at him. He gave no smile of welcome, not even the slightest nod to acknowledge his presence, just an unbroken stare through steel grey eyes. He was not a big man, but he immediately demanded attention - perhaps through his apparent lack of emotion. His lean but powerful-looking body was clothed in immaculate Italian designer clothes, quite out of place for the setting. Dapper, tough, and possibly gay was Harry's instinctive snapshot.

He was not given to making snap judgements like this, and his natural optimism meant that he did not normally take instant dislikes. But in the case of this man, he found himself making an exception.

His companion must have heard Harry's approach for he rose from his chair and turned to greet him. In sharp contrast, his grin seemed to reach from ear to ear. He was immense and approached Harry with arms open wide for a bear-like hug.

Into Harry's mind flashed the memory of a story he had heard some years earlier of such a bear hug from Giovanni. One of his gang leaders had been caught creaming off some of the Firm's money and had been called in to see his boss. His plea that it was needed for his sickly wife and would be paid back in time seemed to fall on responsive ears, for they had known each other for many years. Eventually, Giovanni opened his arms offering a hug of forgiveness, which was accepted with visible relief. Very soon, however, the poor guy was struggling for breath as the hug's pressure grew and grew. As his struggling increased, Giovanni used his enormous strength to squeeze his victim's waist and bend his upper body backwards. Then, in one swift movement, he dropped to the floor, forcing the man's back over his bent knee until, by driving it down relentlessly, some part of it cracked and his broken body lay writhing in agony on the floor. After a while, Giovanni's compassion led to a bullet in the head, and later even stretched to a small pension for his not-so-sick widow. Harry knew that Giovanni certainly had the strength, but he had no idea whether such a thing was anatomically possible. Eyewitnesses had sworn that it had indeed happened but, whatever the truth, the story had in no way diminished Giovanni's stature and respect.

Giovanni wore his sixty-eight years well. His massive body still contained a good proportion of muscle and, although his leg joints were beginning to feel the burden of carrying it, he remained remarkably agile. His round head was perhaps a little small for his frame, although this impression may have been due to its lack of hair. Having begun to lose it very early, he had once invested in a toupee but had burned it within a week when he learned of the secret laughter it was producing. All that survived now was a fringe of grey stubble framing his head. Belying his name, all signs of any swarthy Sicilian blood had long since been laundered out over the generations. This left him resembling a kindly rich uncle, an impression that was enhanced by the ready smile that naturally inhabited his face much of the time. But it was a smile that could vanish in a flash, as Harry knew full well. Throughout his life, both enemies and underlings alike feared him and, although he may no longer be that hands-on hard man, even today you would dare to cross him at your peril.

"Ciao, Harry. Che piacere vederti". Harry smiled to himself. He remembered how Giovanni always started every meeting with some form of greeting in Italian - presumably to underline his family's links with the old country. In fact, he was thoroughly American and Harry doubted that he spoke much Italian at all. "Say, let me introduce you to Carl Fossen."

His companion did manage a slight nod to acknowledge the introduction and even the merest suggestion of a short smile. No hand was offered, however, so Harry just replied in kind.

"Come on Harry. Sit down." Giovanni rearranged the chairs so that Harry was sitting at the end of the table between himself and Fossen. "Good journey?" he asked.

"Yes. Fine thanks. Sorry, I'm a bit late. Hey Giovanni, it's really good to see you again after all this time."

"It's been much too long, Harry. Tell me, how's Tatyana?" This question immediately illustrated the bond between the two men. By all normal Mafia rules and customs, Giovanni should have executed Tatyana along with the other members of her gang. He had not done so because he knew that Harry had fallen for her and that they were already in a relationship. And it was Harry who had just saved his life.

"She's fine, Giovanni. Can we talk later?" Harry asked.

"Yeah. Listen, Harry, straight to business, eh? We'll have dinner later, and jaw into the night. OK, Harry?"

The Englishman smiled to himself once more. He recalled how Giovanni always peppered conversations with the name of the person to whom he was talking - an odd habit, but not unattractive.

Giovanni clearly expected no response, but it was several seconds before he started. "Aw, Harry. Things just ain't like the old days. Maybe they never was. I keep thinking it's my age, but I know it ain't just me. The whole world has changed so much, and with accountants and computer geeks now running the outfit, I simply can't operate as I once did. I used to be able to make every decision myself... and act on it on the spot if necessary. I had the power of life and death in these paws." He spread out a huge pair of hands to underline he point.

"Now, everything has to be considered and agreed by committees." After a short pause and a sigh, he continued, "and these then usually call for a whole bunch of studies - feasibility, likely outcome, possible consequences - by the money men, by lawyers, even fucking public relations people. And so it goes on; drives me crazy, Harry"

"Carl here's a result of all this. Aw - he's a nice enough guy," Giovanni paused, "I'm sure," he added and glanced swiftly at Carl to see if he would accept this as the mild joke that was intended. He did not appear to do so.

"Carl is my shadow - my minder if you like. He's here to make sure I don't say or do anything I shouldn't. Eh, Carl?"

Again, he looked at Carl and once again there was no reaction.

After a moment's silence, he started again, "I don't know if you've heard about my kid brother's health?" Harry shook his head. "He's dying, Harry. It's just a matter of weeks now." Harry noticed the dew forming in the corner of Giovanni's eyes. He knew how very close the brothers were and was genuinely shocked at the news, and also surprised that he had not read of it in the newspapers.

Their father, the ancient Capo, had finally died five years earlier after a long struggle with ill health. The leadership had been a straight choice between Giovanni and his brother, Riccardo. Although he was several years younger, Riccardo had always been the brighter star of the new generation. He had enormous charisma, a razor-sharp intellect, and prodigious organizational powers. He even had the cheek to be better looking than his older brother. Over the years, Giovanni had come to accept all this and had almost always deferred to him, and he had done so once again - "for the sake of the family".

Riccardo had thus been chosen unopposed and had performed brilliantly throughout his term. Under his strong but thoughtful guidance, the Firm followed the worldwide trend towards multi-nationalism and become more truly universal. Before his reign, many countries in the world, particularly those in Eastern Europe, had operated independently. And even in America, there had been constant bickering and dramatic clashes between rival gangs. These had largely been patched up, and although the individual organizations in the larger countries had retained most of their independence, they had generally come to accept, and even welcome, the fact they were all part of a worldwide family.

This news of Riccardo's imminent early death was certain to be a great blow to the Firm. From what Giovanni had said earlier, Harry could well imagine the committees that would still be examining how the news should be released.

"I'm so sorry, Giovanni. You were very close to him, weren't you?" said Harry.

"Yup. We were great buddies as kids, and we stayed that way pretty well throughout. It never once crossed my mind that he'd be the first to go."

After a short while and a heavy sigh, he continued, "Now, we're gonna need a new Capo, and this time it ain't going to be so damned easy." He paused, maybe for effect, or perhaps just to clear his thoughts. "All the bosses from around the world will be at Riccardo's funeral, and soon after it they'll all be meeting to choose a successor - a bit like they do for a new Pope, but no fucking chimney or coloured smoke."

"Anyone who wants to be considered has to stick his head up above the parapet, and there's already been a lot of jockeying for position. Originally there were five or six Americans, but most of them found little support and they've dropped out. There's an Italian - Sicilian background like my own family. But I've heard he's having trouble, even with his own people."

"So at the moment, Harry, we have three front runners. There's Joe Becker from Chicago. He's got a lot of support from the East and Central. He's... OK, I guess". This was said with little conviction, and with some pursing of the lips and a twisting movement of the hands. Not OK at all, Harry thought, and not for the first time he wondered how much Giovanni's words were tempered by Fossen's presence.

"But for a start, he ain't family. And that means quite a lot still. Not just to us, but to most of the older folks. He's also a bit wild - a bit of a firebrand. I'm not too sure. I know a few who'll not be voting for him."

"But the real joker in the pack, Harry, is one of the Russian bosses, a guy called Viktor Rubeliev." Giovanni paused. "Now, he's gotten three things against him. He ain't family, he ain't even American, and he's a

Ruskie! And a fourth even - he seems to have gotten some sort of lead..."

"I know. I know. You're thinking 'What the hell's a Ruskie doing in the frame at all? They're a totally different breed.' And you're right - the Bratva I think they call themselves. Well, many years ago now they started to set up shop in the States. That led to a lot of fighting of course and eventually..." his voice trailed off.

"Well, truth is, we hooked up with this large group of them, mainly to stop us getting at each other's throats all the time. Some of us didn't like it, but Riccardo was keen and, in the end... anyways, it's gotten us into this mess right now."

"And so, Harry, you're looking at the third sucker. I've chucked my hat into the ring. I'm not so sure I'm up to it at my age, but I can't just stand by and let this Ruskie in by default. I gotta put up some sort of fight."

"Trouble is, Harry, he's still gaining more and more support - not just on this side of the pond, but even Stateside too." Giovanni paused for several seconds, wondering how to continue. Eventually, he decided on a direct assault. "We've simply gotta eliminate him from the contest, Harry. There's no other way." After another pause, "And that's where you come in, my good friend..." Giovanni said with a weak smile.

Harry said nothing. He was utterly stunned. Throughout the whole story, he simply had not seen it coming. He was being contracted to assassinate a Russian Mafia boss!

Maybe he should have been flattered. Perhaps he would have been, but he simply couldn't believe Giovanni was being serious. Perhaps he had simply misunderstood what was being asked of him. Harry was not short of confidence - several years in a minor public school and a commission in the Army had taken care of that. But this was surely totally out of his league. He began to laugh and to search for the right form of words for a polite refusal.

But Carl Fossen wasn't laughing with him, and Giovanni now also adopted the man's stony gaze. They both simply stared at him, waiting for his reaction, adding no flesh to the proposal. The laughter soon died from Harry's face. They were deadly serious.

"Giovanni," Harry just smiled now, as he began his protest. "What on earth makes you think I could tackle a job like that?"

With no answer forthcoming he continued, "Listen, you may have my name listed under the heading of 'assassins' in your filing cabinet, but you surely need a professional for this sort of thing – you can't be short of them, for Christ's sake. I don't have the experience for this. I'm just a school teacher who's helped out a mate a couple of times, small-scale stuff – nothing like this."

As an afterthought, he added, "And anyway, I'd never get it past Tatyana when I get home..."

"Harry. Harry. I know, it's a big ask. You're gonna need some time to think it over. But, frankly, time ain't something we have too much of right now." He reached into his chest pocket, took out a pack of Marlborough, tapped out a cigarette and grabbed it between his lips. Leaning to one side, he fished out a chunky Zippo lighter from his trouser pocket, snapped open a large flame, put it to the cigarette and drew the smoke deep into his lungs.

"You're right of course, Harry. We could do it ourselves. But if it ever got out - if anybody ever made the connection…" He blew out his cheeks and left the consequences hanging in the now smoky mid-air.

"But this guy must have the strongest sort of security around him, so how the hell would I get anywhere near him?" Harry demanded. "OK. I've had to tail my prey, but this sort of thing is way outside my area of knowledge and experience."

Almost wearily, Giovanni held up a hand and dismissed these protests, "All it needs is good preparation and common sense. It's not rocket science, Harry. I've seen you in action. You're very handy with all types of weapons, and you know how to look after yourself … and yer mates!" he added pointedly.

Then, after a short pause, he continued, "One thing that might persuade you, Harry. The money! I think you'll agree we always pay top dollar, eh? Well, this one's something else. I accept that." He drew heavily on his cigarette. The smoke escaped from both his mouth and nose as he drawled slowly, "Have you ever thought about giving it all up, Harry?"

Giovanni's question shook him. His great friend had been killed during their last job, several years back, and he had promised Tatyana that he was finished with it.

"I already have, Giovanni. Listen, I was just helping out my best friend. Together, we'd learned to kill in Iraq, but he was following in the footsteps of his father. It must have been in his blood, but it was never in mine and I always knew I wasn't cut out for the job. You were there when he was killed, and that was it as far as I was concerned. Finished!"

"Come on, Harry. You'd surely like to secure a pile for you and Tatyana. We'll pay you very well for a job like this. Five hundred grand up front," he paused, "and then, when we get confirmation that the job's been completed, another two and a half million - that's three big ones in all, Harry". He sat back in his chair, took another long draw on his cigarette and waited for a favourable reaction. "Buy you a good annuity..." he added teasingly.

"Pounds Sterling, Giovanni?" Harry suggested.

This drew a loud laugh from Giovanni, who threw his head back and then slapped Harry on the back, "Dollars, Harry, United States Dollars!" he insisted. Then, with a swift look at Carl, he added, "But I guess everything's negotiable".

"And all expenses?"

"Of course."

Harry remained silent, amazed to hear himself even bothering to negotiate. But he was being offered the chance of setting the two of them up for life. He could not simply ignore it.

The two men continued to stare expectantly at him. "I can't believe I'm even considering it." He said numbly. "I need more information, and more time to think."

"Sure, Harry. But, as I say, time's in short supply right now."

Then he added, "I'm going to leave you with Carl now. He has a fat dossier on Viktor Rubeliev - you know, all the gen we have on his business and family life, his daily movements, his strengths and weaknesses etc. etc. See what you think. We'll talk tonight. Eight o'clock OK?"

As he got up to leave, he dug a card out of his shirt pocket. "Trattoria Vincenzo," he said. "The food's good, and it's quiet and anonymous.

He gave Harry another hug, "It's great to see you again, Harry." Then he turned and said, "Treat him well, Carl. He's a great guy. And give him all you've got". With that, he turned and left Harry to the charms of Carl Fossen.

The weasel by the door remained.

Chapter 3

Viktor Sergei Rubeliev sat back in his oversize chair at his large desk in his vast office reading through the latest reports. Occasionally, he would lean forward to highlight some important text. The scale of everything made him look rather small and insignificant, but he was anything but that. Just over six feet tall with a muscular body, swarthy, with a mop of jet black hair, he was good-looking in that angular Russian sort of way. And an air of authority was stamped on his every movement.

The area to the left of his desk was mostly taken up by a large conference table, with chairs for some twenty or so people. To his right was an area for the more relaxed meetings with armchairs and a couple of sofas, along with a drinks cabinet and even an open fire, unlit at the moment. The door in front of his desk was every bit of twenty feet away and led to his private secretary and administration team. Beyond them was the factory floor. It was a genuine business manufacturing compressors for refrigerators and air conditioning units, a respected and profit-making concern of which Viktor was both its Chief Executive and Chairman.

Beside the sitting area was a spacious bathroom. Viktor would occasionally stay overnight when one of the sofas would double as a reasonably comfortable bed.

Immediately behind his desk a further door led into a private courtyard approached directly from the main road through a secure and manned gateway. It was used exclusively by Viktor and his invited guests, and it was a sharp buzz from this entrance that interrupted Viktor's reading and turned his thoughts immediately to the unpleasant meeting that was slated for the morning.

He opened the left-hand top drawer and pressed one of a block of four buttons. This unlocked the door and Viktor got up to turn and greet his guests as they entered.

Vladimir Mussorgsky headed up the Moscow unit and acted very much as Viktor's right-hand man. He too sported a head of thick black hair, but any likeness ended there. He was a much shorter man and his face, whilst it contained all the necessary features, was curiously nondescript. Consciously or not, he dressed in a manner to accentuate this inconspicuous appearance. He and Viktor had grown up together, served their Bratva apprenticeships together, blooded themselves together with difficult and dangerous tasks, and worked their respective ways up the Organisation together.

He entered first and introduced Viktor to the striking blonde woman that accompanied him. Viktor had met her on several occasions and greeted her warmly.

Olga Pudovkin had founded and was once the Chief Executive of the largest computer software companies in Russia. It had grown very rapidly under her youthful energy and talents, but it was this very youth that had led her to lose more and more control to establishment Party Members who were selected to join the Board as the Company had grown in importance to the military. One day, she had a furious row with the Chairman over a new direction he wished to take the Company and had been dismissed the very next day. Shortly afterwards, she had been head-hunted by Vladimir Mussorgsky to beef up the cyber-crime operations which had been losing out to Africa and the Far East over recent years. This had been only partly successful, but she was nevertheless a valued member of Viktor's team.

Olga was in her mid-thirties now. Her pale oval face was framed by a slick of bleached blond hair that curled round wispily at the front to end just under her chin. Although clearly a tough operator, she had an attractively vulnerable appearance that accompanied a slim, athletic body.

It was she who introduced the second man, who Victor had never met, simply as Sholokhov. In sharp contrast to Olga's elegance, this was a shambles of a man - short and overweight, with an unattractive face furnished by oversize bulbous features. Making an effort for today's meeting, he had forced his body into a suit, but it was shabby and ill-fitting. A blue smudge that might be discerned as a serpent's head peeked out from beneath the short cuffs on either side. These drew Viktor's gaze, and he could imagine that on most days, whilst at his solitary work on a computer, the busily tattooed arms would be visible in their full glory, sprouting from some hideous sort of sleeveless t-shirt. Today, none of this was helped by the sweat that was already glistening on his face.

Viktor had read Olga's full report on him the night before, and it had not sent him to sleep in a good mood. As is normal, all personnel operating in this area did so in a series of cells, either as individuals or in very small groups, which were controlled by a trusted Manager who then reported directly to Olga. Sholokhov had unearthed a hoard of usernames and passwords from a retailer's insecure site in the United States and had managed to syphon off several lucrative accounts, informing Olga and depositing the proceeds into defined accounts of the Firm. By coincidence, another cell had chanced upon the same cache. This happened from time to time, and they had not been surprised to find that some of the accounts had already been looted. What did surprise them however was the audit trail which showed that, although two of the accounts had been processed through proper channels, another three ended up in an unknown account in the Dominican Republic.

Olga hauled in Sholokhov, who eventually had to admit that this rogue account was under his control. He made some blustering excuses about it being a temporary holding account set up because of security concerns, but this explanation had been speedily demolished, and he was now being presented to learn the consequences of his betrayal.

This was no informal meeting and the three sat on chairs in front of Viktor's desk as they talked around the facts of the case, Sholokhov was very pale and constantly played with his hands.

"You have to believe me; I would have transferred the money into one of the Company's funds eventually. I just didn't think it was safe to put it all into one account at once. I'm so sorry. It won't happen again. It was a stupid mistake. I was stupid. Stupid!"

"These accounts have been set up for your use by highly skilled money people, Sholokhov," Rubeliev said. "They are completely secure. You know that perfectly well. You've been using them for years. I don't believe any of your excuses."

Sholokhov was now beside himself and only able to stutter out apologies, "I'm so sorry. I've never done anything like it before. Please, Mr Rubeliev. I can be very useful to the Organisation. Please..."

Viktor nodded to Vladimir who then got up and went through to the bathroom. "I'm sorry too, Sholokhov. Miss Pudovkin tells me you were starting to become a very useful asset. She had great hopes for your future." He paused then, apparently deep in thought. "But when you act in this manner, all trust is gone. It cannot go unpunished. You know this."

Vladimir returned and stood by the bathroom door. Viktor stood up. "Follow me please," he said brusquely. They all followed him into the bathroom where a hidden doorway had been opened, and which led into another small office. This room had been constructed in the utmost secrecy by Viktor's predecessor at the time the factory was first built. It was not marked on any plans and only a very detailed survey of the whole premises would reveal its existence. There were no windows. It was frugally furnished with a couple of filing cabinets, a few chairs and a desk to which Viktor headed. Opposite the desk was an odd-looking industrial type of armchair, to which Sholokhov was led.

As he sat down, metal clamps emerged from beneath the arms and swept up and over Sholokhov's hands, locking them to the chair frame. Similar clamps opened from underneath, securing both his legs. He was now sweating profusely and deathly pale.

Viktor leant forward and pressed a button on yet another block, this time on the top of the desk. With a faint *click,* a flap in the ceiling opened and then, with a loud whirring noise, a device descended on a steel rod which consisted mainly of two somewhat larger clamps. These forced themselves around the head of Sholokhov, who was by now utterly terrified. The clamps closed and jerked his head to face straight ahead, and locked it firmly in position.

"Now," said Viktor. "I'm sure I that I have your full attention." After a short pause, he continued, "Your guilt has been proved to me. It just remains to establish whether anyone else is involved. You've told Miss Pudovkin that you were acting entirely alone, but I am not convinced."

"Now, from my experience, persons who find themselves in your current predicament tend to become more enthusiastic about telling the truth. Am I right, Sholokhov?"

Words began to pour from the terrified man, an almost incomprehensible mixture of apologies and excuses. Viktor held up a hand. "We're way past all that, Sholokhov. I want to know who else knew of this account of yours. You have a girlfriend I understand?"

"She knew nothing," said Sholokhov, almost wearily. "She's just a girl. I've never talked to her about my work or anything..." His voice tailed off, as he began to sob quietly.

Viktor thought for a moment. He looked at his friend Vladimir, who gave a gentle nod. "I have to believe you," said Viktor finally as he reached for another of the buttons.

More whirring began, but this time the whole apparatus revolved rapidly through 360 degrees once, twice, six times taking Sholokhov's head with it. After only a couple of turns, the spinal cord cracked open and the soft tissue and flesh of the neck spiralled freely into a plaited knot. Arteries ruptured and streams of blood started pumping out through skin torn open by pieces of bone. Spurts of blood splattered the walls, ceiling and furniture. Rubeliev calmly brushed away a couple of spots that landed on his hand.

When it stopped, Sholokhov was still facing Viktor with huge eyes staring, but gone was all the terror he had shown earlier, replaced now by just a look of sheer surprise.

Olga Pudovkin cried out and rushed to the bathroom. Both Viktor and Vladimir remained silent, almost respectful. Finally, Rubeliev reached for another button which released the clamps holding Sholokhov's head which then flopped onto his chest and lay there, lolling slightly as the rest of his body continued to twitch.

The two men had witnessed the scene on more than one occasion. These were tough men, and such scenes of violence had been commonplace throughout their adult lives. Nevertheless, Viktor at least could not claim to be unmoved. He was reminded of his ex-boss, from whom he had inherited this machine of interrogation and death. He had little in common with that very violent man, and more than once he had considered dismantling and destroying it. But then, how would he replace it? Although such events were thoroughly distasteful, occasions would always arise when something of the sort would be required. The machine did its job, he had always decided, and he would keep it for now.

The two men looked at each other. Viktor sighed and said, "I'm going to do a round of the factory, Vova. Would you arrange the usual please?" Vladimir nodded, and Viktor slapped him lightly on his back as he strode out, certain that his friend had already arranged for a clean-up team to be standing by.

It had become almost a ritual after such an event for Viktor to make a tour of the factory floor. It seemed to relax him, talking to foremen and assembly line staff alike, identifying and discussing any problems that had arisen. He had always taken an active interest in the business, even if he did not have the time to be exactly hands-on.

It was the best part of an hour before he returned to his office. The bathroom door was closed, and he knew that behind it everything would be spotless and back in its normal condition. It was a moment or two before he spotted that one thing at least was out of place - Olga Pudovkin. She was still in his office, lying on one of the settees.

He went over to her. "Are you alright?" he asked. "I'm so sorry. I should have realised and warned you. I guess you're more used to computers dying on you, eh?" he added, trying to introduce a lighter note.

She said nothing but began to sob once again. Maybe it was the sight of her vulnerability but, as she unfurled her long legs to get up from the sofa, Viktor suddenly saw her as an attractive woman - amazingly for the first time in all their meetings. She came over to him and sobbed quietly on his shoulder. He could do nothing but put his arms around her, patting her on the back and meekly apologising once more.

Suddenly, he felt her hand slip down his thigh and then rub down his penis, which began to react immediately. That extraordinary warm feeling of heightened excitement coursed involuntary through his body. But this was not right, and he pulled away swiftly. In all the twelve years of his marriage to Elena, he had not once been unfaithful to her, and he was not about to start today, whatever the chemistry within his body was telling him.

However repulsed she had been by what she had witnessed, she had plainly been excited in equal measure. "I'm sorry," she muttered softly as he moved away from her. "No harm done," he said rather brusquely as he strode towards his desk. "I'll arrange for a car to take you home".

Chapter 4

Harry emerged from Gloucester Road Underground Station to one **of** those perfect English spring days. It was early evening, and the whole of London was bathed in warm, dusky Technicolor. He knew that even if a bus did come along soon, at this time of day it could take double the time to make the ten-minute journey. After the plane and train, it would be a pleasure to walk to his house. And besides, it would allow him to consider how he was going to play things with Tatyana.

He recalled how he had foolishly left his plane ticket on his dressing table and the moment when Tatyana had come downstairs looking rather grim. He had realised immediately that she had seen his destination and had made the link with Giovanni and the Mafia. She had said nothing, nor had she quizzed him about any possible new job. But from that moment until he had left the house, she had been very cool and withdrawn. It had not been a happy departure.

Harry realised that, whilst he would have to give her an honest and reasonably full account of Giovanni's offer, he would need to play down the difficulties - in particular the inherent dangers. Some years ago, after the last disastrous assignment in Moscow, he had agreed with Tatyana that there would be no more, and he was certain that she would put up stern resistance to the proposal. His trump card might be to assure her that the high fee would allow him to give it up completely with their future assured. However, she was not stupid and it would also alert her to the magnitude of the dangers involved. The Mafia were always willing to pay well, but they did insist on real value for their money.

He decided he would tell her all about his meetings with Giovanni, his brother's illness, the problems with succession, and the need for an outside operator to get rid of the problematic Russian. He had pretty well got this clear in his head by the time he arrived at the black cast iron gate to their small two-storey townhouse.

Harry had been expecting a cool reception that would mirror his departure. But when Tatyana opened the door she was beaming. "Harry," she cried excitedly and threw her arm around him dragging him over the threshold. Whatever she was wearing, Harry could feel that it was very little, and he only just managed to hook the front door shut before she began forcing him to the floor. As he fell, his case slipped from his hand and hit something with a bang. He glanced over to see if anything was damaged, but she was on top of him like a wildcat tearing off his jacket and unzipping his flies. He could see her breasts rising and falling under a thin blouse as she pounded into him. Her face, partly concealed by her long blond hair, was gorged and contorted as she sucked in some air.

It was over all too soon, but they remained locked together breathing heavily. "Welcome home, Harry," she cried, which started them both laughing. After several minutes, Harry withdrew himself from her. "Good trip?" she asked, and they started laughing again. It was an excellent homecoming.

As she went upstairs to shower, still chuckling, Harry just lay there for a while without even bothering to cover his nakedness. It was now more than three years since fate had thrown them together in remarkable and dangerous circumstances. Their liaison had been very nearly strangled at birth, but this very fact may have deepened and strengthened their bond. Both still resented every moment they were apart.

In some of their more intimate moments, Harry would call her "Angel", in part because that is how he would describe her. Perhaps her face would not be classed as classically beautiful, but it was devastatingly pretty and her lively personality shone brightly through it. Framed by a mass of gently curling blond hair, a small slightly turned-up nose was perched beneath startling blue eyes that looked out at the world with confidence and optimism. Even in repose, her lips seemed to wear the hint of a smile and she attracted the stares of men and wolf whistles from the lads wherever she went. Each morning, as Harry's eyes caught sight of her on the pillow beside him, a lurch in his stomach reminded him of his great good fortune.

Eventually, he got up leaving most of his clothes where they lay, and went to the downstairs toilet to clean himself off. He returned to the hall to discover that nothing had been broken by his case, just a dent in the skirting board. By the time he had picked up his clothes and case, she was coming down the stairs.

"I'll go and have a shower now, darling," he said.

"That's good," she said with a smile and a pursing of her nose. "G and T?" and then added, "Outside?"

"Please. I won't be long".

Half an hour later, on their terrace, he felt remarkably relaxed. The warm evening sun on his face, the gin and the woman he loved, all combined to make yesterday afternoon's awkward meeting with Carl Fossen seem a million years ago. They talked of the weather and the tragic shooting in the American school. And she told him of her latest purchases. They talked of anything but his trip.

This prevarication continued well into dinner until, whilst she was still making the coffee, Tatyana leant back against the worktop and opened with the first salvo. "So," she asked. "How was Giovanni?"

Harry took it in his stride. "Fine! Still the big bear," he laughed, perhaps a bit nervously. "He must be nearly seventy, you know."

"Yes," she said and then paused, waiting for him to continue. When he remained silent, she continued, "And he'd called you over just for two friends to chat over old times. Was that it?"

He smiled wryly. "Well, we certainly did quite a bit of that, darling. We had dinner together last night. He wanted to know all about you and what we'd been doing. And he sends his love, of course." He paused, but her silent stare forced him to continue. "No. He did offer me a little job. It's got to be done fairly soon, so it fits in nicely." They were booked for a safari holiday in a few weeks.

Silence hung heavily in the air, until finally, "Harry! For fuck's sake, tell me about it..."

Her evident frustration was now verging on anger, and Harry realised that real hostilities had finally broken out. She could keep her somewhat volatile East European temperament in check for only so long, and he could not afford to antagonise her further.

"OK. OK," he started. Then, after a short pause, "It's a job they feel they can't do themselves - for political reasons." He proceeded to give her a straightforward account of his meetings with Giovanni and Fossen. When he had finished there was another of those uncomfortable silences. But she had a look on her lovely face that Harry had seen a few times before, and he knew that a storm was about to break. He was certain then that he had not got away with it.

"So," she said finally. "All you have to do is to nip over to Moscow and assassinate one of Russia's Mafia bosses. It's as simple as that, eh? Just a few days' work - might even get time for a bit of sightseeing. It could be fun." She paused for a while, gathering momentum. "Tell me, Harry, is it just a pleasure trip they're laying on for you?" And after another short pause, "or will they by any chance be paying you for this?"

Harry was acutely aware that this was now crunch time. He was certain that she was questioning the size of the paycheck to gauge the magnitude of the dangers involved. But it was something he had no way of dodging.

"Now listen, darling," he began. "I know what you're thinking. It's no small job - I admit it. But I promise you I won't be doing it if I don't think it can be done safely."

He paused as Tatyana stood with arms akimbo, just staring at him. He continued, "You think I'm an amateur, don't you? I should never have gone in with

Bob." He sighed and then, "I often wonder why I did myself. It just seemed right at the time."

With a shrug he added, "And you're right, of course. I'm just a sports jock, turned school teacher. What the hell am I doing?"

Again he sighed. "But you know it was the Army that taught me how to kill. There's no Academy for assassins. It doesn't need years of study - just a little experience, some knowledge of weapons and sheer common sense." Harry found himself using Giovanni's arguments. "Bob and I did a couple of jobs very successfully."

"My God, Harry. Don't you see the difference? That last one was a nasty little man of no consequence. The world is well rid of him. We're talking here of a Mafia boss – a tough man, probably violent, with loads of protection, surrounded by security at all times. What the hell are you thinking of?"

Harry had no answer. The previous contracts had paid well, allowing them both to enjoy a reasonably comfortable and carefree life. But he had put up no fight when Tatyana had insisted that it should finish.

"You're not doing it," she said softly, but emphatically.

"Look. I talked about it at length with Giovanni yesterday evening. You know he feels indebted to me, Tania. There's no way he would ask me to do anything he thought I couldn't do successfully and survive." Then, after a pause, he felt it was time to play his trump card. "Anyway, we eventually negotiated a fee that would be large enough to set us up for life - pack it all in, once and for all. That's what you want, isn't it darling?"

"Don't 'darling' me. That's what we agreed three years ago."

Harry said nothing.

"You're not doing it, Harry. And that's that." Again, she spoke quietly, but with an air of absolute finality, as she got up and headed for the door.

"Too late, I'm afraid. I've already agreed with Giovanni," he shouted after her.

"Then you'd better get in touch with him and un-agree it." Tatyana shouted back after she had already left the room.

The subject was not mentioned again during the whole of that desultory evening. They talked little. Harry tried to relieve some of the tension by playing a couple of their favourite TV programmes he had recorded, but they were in bed before eleven o'clock. They kissed briefly, but then turned away from each other in the bed.

Sleep did not come easily to either of them, each with their own thoughts. Tatyana found herself reliving the other sleepless nights when Harry was away on a job. She dreaded the idea of adding to them.

As she tried to put it from her mind, her thoughts turned to her early life and the circumstances that eventually led to her first meeting with this man she loved so much.

Chapter 5

Tatyana was born near Makhachkala, the capital city of the Republic of Dagestan, a self-governing state within the old Russian Empire. She had enjoyed an idyllic childhood in a large house on the banks of the Caspian Sea. Her parents were both Russian by birth and were part of the privileged class in a country divided by a huge variety of ethnic groups, all vying for influence and power. Her mother was a prominent lawyer and her father an industrialist and local politician, tipped for higher office by many. She was educated in private girls' schools and emerged as a popular beauty, ready to take her place at university.

She could have taken up places offered by several good universities in Russia, including a couple in Moscow. But she was proud of the State of Dagestan and wished to remain close to her parents, so she eventually decided on a local college. This proved to be unfortunate because it was here that she met and fell in love with Mukhu, a man of the Kumyk ethnic group. He was an ardent supporter of independence for Dagestan and soon became the leader of a group of dissidents which became more and more militant under his influence.

Tatyana had naturally become a member of this group and an increasingly political animal. This did not please her parents who were comfortable with the status quo - quite content with the state within a state situation. Nor did they approve of Mukhu, who they considered to be a dangerous influence on their only child.

Their fears were realised in the long holiday of the second year when Mukhu decided that the time had come to publicise their cause to a wider audience, and planned for his core group of militants to spend the summer vacations in Moscow. By this time, his aggression had reached new levels, and he had managed to acquire some guns to take with them, a Kalashnikov automatic for himself and a variety of handguns for the remainder of his group, including Tatyana. They travelled together on the long train journey and then settled down to make their plans in a cheap hotel in the suburbs.

It may have been this new violent attitude but, for whatever reason, it was not long before there was a tangible blunting of the couple's affections. He no longer sought out her company but treated her as just one of his foot soldiers. For her part, she was happy to let this ride and made no move to get closer to him. Moreover, she began to have serious reservations about the direction they seem to be going. This was raised to a level of considerable alarm when he announced that he planned to kidnap for ransom a high-profile American lawyer, who he had read in a newspaper was visiting Moscow. This, he insisted, would give them great publicity both in the East and the West, and at the same time raise some much-needed finance for their cause.

Tatyana did not wish to get involved with this and toyed with the idea of returning to Dagestan. But she had become afraid of Mukhu by now, who she felt had become an unpredictable and rather vicious character, and who was moving further and further away from the man she had once loved. He may have detected this, for he left her out of the kidnap operation itself, and put her in charge of caring for their captive. They planned to keep him in the basement of a deserted warehouse they had fitted out with a bed, some chairs and a few other essentials. Whilst the others would carry out all the security and guarding arrangements, she was to arrange for all the man's needs for the duration of his captivity, which it was hoped would not be too long.

The capture itself was well enough planned and was achieved without hitch. It was only later that some other members of the gang began to perceive the whole venture as premature and amateurish. Indeed, from the moment the poor American was installed in their hiding place, Mukhu did not seem to have any real idea how to extract any publicity from him. The hijacking was reported of course, but became yesterday's news very quickly in the face of other world events. Mukhu wrote to several newspapers claiming that the lawyer was being held by his Independence for Dagestan Group, and demanding a ransom of fifty million roubles. Nobody had heard of them and probably did not believe it was genuine. No ransom offer was ever made.

After nothing had happened for several days, the group became very agitated. Their captive was probably the most composed amongst them, assuring them of his support for their cause and offering to take no action if they released him somewhere in Moscow, an offer that more than just Tatyana would have liked to consider. But Mukhu stood firm.

One evening, whilst he was planning more letters to the newspapers, Tatyana decided she needed some space and went out to the area's only decent hotel bar for a drink. And it was there that she first met Harry.

She had bought herself a beer and was sitting at the bar when two men entered and settled on stools a discrete distance away from her. More than five minutes passed before Harry detached himself from his friend and came over to stand by her. He introduced himself, rather formally Tatyana thought, "I'm Harry Fletcher. Are you staying at this hotel?"

She had replied not, but in a friendly manner, which he had taken as permission to sit on the stool next to her. They talked and he bought her a glass of wine, more to her usual taste. Being with Mukhu, she had learned to drink beer only because it was a cheaper option. After a little while, Harry's friend had come over and shook hands with Tatyana, introducing himself as Bob. He slapped Harry on the back saying he would see him later, and limped out of the bar. They talked some more, and he then took her into the hotel restaurant for dinner.

Harry was something very different from any of her previous experiences. Whilst Mukhu had the classic swarthy "pretty boy" looks that young girls dream of, Harry was a tall man with pale English skin. He had a generous wide mouth underneath a nose that was rather too long, but which gave him a certain aristocratic appearance. His head was topped by a thick mop of curly dark brown hair, which could alter his looks depending on the time of day. In the morning, for instance, these wild curls would fight a losing battle in a vain attempt to recover from the sleeping hours, and it was to be only a couple of days before she was to witness this.

They became good friends as well as lovers, meeting up whenever the slightest possibility arose. Harry had introduced himself as an Agricultural Consultant employed by the local Cooperative to help many farms, but it was several days before Tatyana told him about their group. When she did, however, her extreme anxiety about the kidnapping caused her to go well beyond what she had planned, and to reveal the whole story. Harry had been shocked and dismayed, but sympathetic about her opposition to it. He said that he knew people who could help if she would tell him where the lawyer was being held. Torn between the wish to resolve the problem and her loyalty to Mukhu and his group, she refused to tell him for some time, but Harry continued to ask her most persuasively, and she eventually succumbed.

What no one in this sad little group had any means of knowing was that this particular lawyer was in the pay of the US Mafia, and more particularly of Giovanni Pollini. His courtroom skills had saved Giovanni from prison on more than one occasion, and when he heard of the man's kidnapping, he had taken personal charge of their rescue effort.

The Moscow police and other Russian authorities were having no success in discovering the identities of the kidnappers, nor did their counterparts in Dagestan seem able to help. However, the long fingers of the Mafia reached into their home town and a slice of luck gave Giovanni the identity of Mukhu's outfit, which eventually led to news of their journey to Moscow.

Rather than immediately setting sail with his own crew into foreign lands, Giovanni decided to make use of Bob and Harry to discover where the lawyer was being held. He planned to then join them to make the rescue, and to exact the usual Mafia retribution for those who harm their own.

As soon as he received the news that the hideaway had been discovered, Giovanni set off with two of his best men. On the very day of their arrival, they joined up with Bob and Harry to inspect the site from the outside and decided that the raid should take place the following evening.

To make sure she was not present, Harry arranged to meet Tatyana in the bar of his hotel at the agreed time of the raid.

The five of them crashed through the door of the warehouse with guns drawn and surprised four of the gang playing cards. To the horror of Harry and Bob, Giovanni and his men showed no mercy from the moment they entered. Each of the men was despatched with bullets to his head long before he had time to retrieve his own weapon, or even to raise his hands in surrender.

Thinking that the rescue was already over, Harry went over to a bed in the corner on which the lawyer was lying quietly.

Suddenly, however, he heard a loud noise and turned to see Mukhu entering through another door, hidden by a crude screen. He immediately started firing with an automatic rifle and Harry cried out as he saw

Bob fall under a hail of bullets. As Mukhu started to turn his gun towards Giovanni, Harry raised his gun and shot him once, twice, three times in the head. The man's whole body jerked backwards with his Kalashnikov firing bursts of stray bullets harmlessly into the walls and ceiling.

Giovanni grimly walked over to him and put another couple of rounds into his heart. He had not said anything at the time but was naturally acutely aware that Harry's accurate shooting had saved his life. Harry never mentioned it, of course, but it remained a debt that Giovanni would attempt to repay in a number of instalments during his lifetime.

The whole incident was over within a couple of minutes. It caused very little local stir, with the lawyer rapidly returning to the States without explanation or any formal investigation. The authorities were embarrassed by their failure to act in any way, and the whole episode was allowed to be forgotten. The remaining two Dagestans managed to evade Giovanni's retribution, but only for a while. Within six months, they both went missing, the only evidence of their fate being the severed head of one of them found in his parent's deep freeze.

Harry, however, was left grieving for his best friend. Moreover, he had the problem of disposing of his body, those of the others having been unceremoniously dumped in a lake by Giovanni's men. He eventually arranged for a quiet cremation and took the ashes back to England where he and his sister later held a small memorial service.

Immediately following the rescue operation, however, Harry was concerned about Tatyana's safety. He had already explained to Giovanni that she was a member of the gang only through her relationship with Mukhu and that she had tried to prevent the kidnapping. Also, it was she who had provided the whereabouts of the hideaway. Giovanni had said nothing, but nodded his head enigmatically, in quiet thought. Harry hoped he had read him correctly.

Immediately after the raid, he had left the professionals to clean the place up and dispose of the bodies, along with any evidence. Tatyana was still waiting at the hotel bar and was so relieved to see him. His excuses for being so late paled into insignificance beside the news that he then had to break to her. He began with a simple account of the raid, and the massacre by Giovanni and his Mafia squad. She burst into tears of course, and Harry did his best to console her, thankful that the bar was practically empty.

It was several minutes before she regained any semblance of composure but, as she did so, a strange look of incomprehension came over her face.

"What were you doing there, Harry?" she asked through her tears.

This was neither the time nor the place that he had planned for the inevitable confession he would have to make, but he had no choice now.

Tatyana listened grimly as Harry narrated the whole story from the time Giovanni had first contacted Bob. Her tears dried up, replaced by mounting anger as she began to understand how she had been used. Yes, Harry finally accepted, his first contact with her had been planned, and he could understand her anger and disappointment, but he swore to her that their romance had not been a lie. "You must believe me," he insisted. "I couldn't help myself. You must know it. You must surely feel how deeply I have fallen for you."

He leaned forward to take her hand, but she pulled it away saying brusquely, "Don't touch me." Harry's heart sank.

Despite his efforts over the next couple of days, she refused to see him. One evening, she entered the bar where Giovanni and Harry were sitting. As she went to order a drink, Giovanni told Harry to get lost and moved over to buy the drink for her. He led her over to a quiet table in the corner and told her at length of Harry's misery. He had been very persuasive and she had listened with tears in her eyes.

Finally, he gave her an ultimatum. "Tatyana, my dear, you've got only a couple of choices to make. You can forgive him the way you two met, and accept the bond that's formed between you – and I do believe you feel it too." He paused to let this option sink in, and then continued, "Or, you can dig yer obstinate little heels in, and probably regret it for the rest of yer life. In that case, I'll buy you a ticket an' you can hightail it back to yer family in Dagestan."

After another pause to underline the point he added. "Think on it well tonight, my dear gal. I'll be here at the same time tomorrow night. Just let me know your decision." He finished his drink, got up, patted her on the head and walked away.

Tatyana must have changed her mind at least a dozen times over the next twenty-four hours, and she was still unsure as she went down to the bar. Giovanni was sitting alone at the same table as the night before and had her favourite drink already waiting for her. He stood up as she approached and waived her to the chair beside him.

"Well m'dear," he said. "You reached a decision?"

"Yes," she replied and paused. "I'm so sorry. You tried hard, and I do believe that Harry will be sad. But I just can't accept the deceit, Giovanni." She started to cry and kept saying, "I'm sorry, I'm sorry" over her tears.

Giovanni did his best to console her. "OK. It's OK. I'll get you a ticket, and you can go back to yer parents tomorrow. In time, I guess you'll both get over it."

Tatyana had gone to sleep that night sobbing, but she did sleep long and deeply having made her decision.

When she finally awoke, she found an envelope under her door. It contained a brief note from Giovanni wishing her luck, a railway ticket to Makhachkala and ten thousand roubles in cash. It was a long journey and she would have to change twice.

She looked at her watch and realised that she was in danger of missing the train. She packed a small bag with her few belongings and hurried to the station, relieved that she would have no time to run into Harry. That relief was short-lived, however, when she saw him standing by the gate to her platform. The train was due to leave and a guard was getting ready to close the gate, but she could not ignore him. She smiled and kissed him briefly on the cheek saying, "I'm so sorry.

Goodbye Harry," and scuttled through the gate and onto the train.

Less than a minute later - it may have been a slight jolt as the train moved off that caused her to change her mind for what was to be the last time. She grabbed her bag and jumped from the already moving train, nearly knocking over a guard who probably saved her from a bad fall.

Harry had seen all this as he gloomily watched the train begin to move away. She looked up to see him grappling with the gateman who was trying in vain to prevent him from entering the platform. They both ran the short distance between them and threw their arms around each other. The guards soon gave up their protests as the two stayed locked together for what seemed minutes. Finally, she pulled away and, with tears streaming down her cheeks, she managed to blurt out, "An English film I think, Harry. A Short Encounter?"

"Yes." Harry laughed nervously and looked at her expectantly. "A brief one indeed. But with a different ending, I hope," he added.

She nodded and laughed, and cried.

It was a scene that Tatyana had re-played in her mind any number of times over the years, but tonight she found that she was still unable to sleep. She turned over in bed but was confronted with Harry's back. She whispered his name, and then again a bit louder. But there was no reply, and she guessed from his steady breathing that he at least had managed to find some sleep.

Chapter 6

The morning promised another bright day. Perversely, the dark hours seemed to have eased the gloomy mood that had enveloped them on the previous evening. Over bowls of yoghurt and cereal, Tatyana asked to be given more information about the job - everything he knew about it. She had not changed her mind, she insisted sternly, but it was only fair that she should at least listen to the whole story. Harry explained that there was not much more to tell - that it was very much up to him to work up a plan, but he was able to give her a few extra details that he had gleaned from his briefing with Carl Fossen.

He then suggested that they should together go through the dossier that Fossen had prepared. He had not yet had an opportunity himself to do more than glance through it. Perhaps together they could form the basis of a plan, or maybe they would come to a joint conclusion that it was indeed all too risky. But an opportunity to secure such a great nest egg surely deserved a more detailed examination.

Tatyana agreed without enthusiasm and, when breakfast was cleared away, they opened up the dossier on the kitchen table. It contained maps, plans and photos of Rubeliev's house on a road off Moscow's Rublevo-Uspenskoe Highway, and of his office where he worked as the CEO of a manufacturing firm some twelve-mile journey from the house. Although it was certainly a genuine job, the Works Manager took the vast majority of day-to-day decisions, freeing time up for his more onerous, but less legitimate, business.

He was away from both home and office a great deal of the time, with meetings all over Russia and the rest of the world. But wherever he was, he was well protected by his security staff around the clock. Some would accompany him, demonstrating a visible sign of protection. Others would carry out their task discreetly with careful monitoring and surveillance at a distance. But in the factory and home, state-of-the-art security measures allowed for a more relaxed regime. Although various authorities had theories and suspicions about his activities, to neighbours at home and to the staff of the factory, he was just a good family man and industrial leader.

He was also a well-educated man, having studied languages at University, and reputedly spoke immaculate English.

Although the Thieves Code of many Russian Mafia groups prohibits all family ties, Rubeliev's was not one of them. He had married Elena just before the turn of the Millennium and was a loving and attentive husband and father of two sons. When not away on business, he would live in their large house as much as possible - like any normal family. This was not possible, of course. Even though it was fully enclosed by high green metal fencing and security cameras, there were always security men around their home. Occasionally, they would venture into the City Centre to a restaurant or theatre, but would always be accompanied by protection. There were some grainy and blurred photographs of him and his family and even some of his suspected security guards.

The dossier also contained schedules detailing the routes Rubeliev took between home and the factory, along with timings. He seemed to prefer to drive himself but was always accompanied by either a friend or security men. As he read this, Harry made a mental note that this may provide one of the best opportunities for him. He would have to check and update this data very carefully on-site.

Then, there was much information about the Mafia's organisation in Russia. Rubeliev was the head, or Pakhan, of just one of many separate criminal organisations in Russia which are for convenience normally lumped together as the Russian Mafia. His being one of the biggest and best organised, American bosses generally recognised Rubeliev as the Russian Mafia's leader, and he had formed a firm personal friendship with Riccardo Pollini.

The Mob's power and influence pervaded the whole of Russia's infrastructure, directly or indirectly affecting almost every aspect of Russian life. It was embedded into every occupation from the highest ranked politicians to the most menial of municipal workers. There were specialist groups of all descriptions - the traditional ones of gambling, drugs, and the sex trade - but various types of cyber-crime now formed one of its larger contributors. All operated in diverse and shadowy cells, and were co-ordinated, controlled and protected from the law authorities through bribery and coercion. And then there were the moneymen who collected and audited the illicit takings, arranging for their laundering though the world's banking systems, and then investing in legitimate businesses.

All this was largely only of peripheral interest to the job in hand, but there was one sheet of paper detailing Rubeliev's immediate staff. His main man was Vladimir Mussorgsky, who also headed up the whole of their Moscow outfit. He was not a high profile figure like Rubeliev but in many ways a tougher character. Although only minor charges had ever been brought against him, it was known that he had presided over many inter-gang killings designed to strengthen the Mob's hold on the upstart criminals who increasingly attempted to muscle in on their territory. Beneath him was a vast infrastructure of Brigadiers, Boyeviks and Shestyorkas – literally gang bosses, their lieutenants and operatives of all descriptions.

Whilst Rubeliev had been born into the higher echelons of the organisation, Mussorgsky's parents were respected members of the medical world. Unfortunately, their work had taken preference over the raising of their only child, and they failed to notice the nature of the company he kept at school. The two of them had become close friends when they joined secondary school at the same time. He had inevitably become drawn into the dark world of Rubeliev's family and friends. Whether or not he was born with a particularly strong sadistic side to his nature, he immediately took on the role of tough guy and was soon the first choice to carry out violent acts as they become necessary. They made a good team. Whilst he accepted that Viktor had the brains, he was happy to be the brawn.

Finally, a separate envelope provided details of the only real assistance that the Americans were prepared to provide. An encrypted section contained an introduction to an independent armourer from whom he could obtain any hardware he might need during the operation. Clearly, with the tight security of modern-day travel, weaponry has become much more difficult to move between countries and is now almost always sourced locally. From this need has sprung up a network of hardware dealers, independent of any particular outfit, who can provide guns, knives, chemicals – in fact, just about any form of lethal weapon – along with a variety of items for other underworld activities. Sometimes referred to generically as armourers, all they require for their services are confidentiality and an exceptional return on their capital outlay.

It became clear that this particular armourer had an arrangement with Giovanni for payment direct, and there were specific instructions that all items provided should, under no circumstances, be returned to the armourer, but should be destroyed or otherwise disposed of after use.

When they had examined all its contents, Harry shuffled the dossier back into its folder with a small sigh and said, "Well, that's all I have for the moment. The next step is to get out there and have a look on the ground."

Tatyana grunted but did not say anything. After a while, she stood up, picked up a piece of paper from the sideboard, and said tersely, "I've got some shopping to do. Otherwise, we won't have anything to eat tonight."

After she had left, a little searching around found Harry's somewhat tattered map of Moscow and he spread it out on the kitchen table. He dug out the larger scale maps from the dossier and took some time acquainting himself with the area generally, and the routes from Rubeliev's house to the factory. Although he had visited Moscow, this was not familiar territory to him.

Tatyana returned at lunchtime and made a ham salad which they ate with a bottle of Rosé wine out on the sunny terrace. Maybe the wine loosened Tatyana's tongue as she started, "I've been thinking. I know how important this job is for you, darling," then after a while, "and if it does provide well enough for you to give it up for good - *for a second time...*" she added pointedly as her voice trailed off and she paused once more.

"I think it's only fair if I let you at least do some reconnoitring on the spot. That is - if you'll agree to stop and abandon the project completely if it is clearly too dangerous." She paused for a moment, and then challenged, "Will you agree to that?"

Harry thought for a minute and then asked, "And who decides if it is too dangerous?"

"I do," she said flatly.

Harry thought some more. She was making an effort to reach some form of accommodation. This new stance undoubtedly stemmed from the money, but would this be a strong enough incentive for her to make a reasoned judgement? After a moment he sighed and said simply, "OK". They exchanged high-fives and kissed to cement the truce.

The relief on her face was plain. "Good," she said, and added swiftly, "Right, arrange a couple of tickets to Moscow and we'll see what it's all about."

She certainly had a sharp sense of theatre, thought Harry. Her words sliced through him like a dagger. He almost felt the pain physically. But he managed to laugh it off, "No. No. No. This is a man's job," he said smiling. And then with a serious face, "any discussion on the subject is ended".

"I'm sorry Harry. That's all part of the deal. How can I possibly judge whether it's too dangerous if I'm not there? And besides, there are other things to consider. A man alone will always be more conspicuous than a loving couple sightseeing," said Tatyana coyly and then added, "and I speak Russian fluently. Yours is a joke! I can actually be a great help to you"

"Tania! I said the discussion is ended - right now." Harry dismissed her suggestion firmly, although he realised that she had made a couple of good points. For her part, Tatyana knew that Harry's mind-set on this was unmovable and reluctantly said nothing more.

Chapter 7

As the domestic negotiations in the Fletcher family house drew to a close, so were others due to open on the other side of the Atlantic.

Giovanni was on his way back from Europe and had decided to break his journey to meet up with Joe Becker in Chicago. He had little time for the man, but the two of them did represent the bulk of the American challenge in the forthcoming contest, and Carl Fossen was insistent that Becker should be kept in the loop regarding their plans for Rubeliev. For different reasons, neither of them trusted the man and did not want him dreaming up some half-baked scheme of his own.

Becker awoke to a heavy grey sky loaded with rain, which threatened to fall over the next few hours. He was a worried man, for he was simply at a loss to understand the events of the last few weeks. When he learned of the terminal nature of Riccardo's illness, he organised his supporters to put his name forward for the job. No choice would be made until after Riccardo's funeral, of course, but the principle contenders needed to be established well before then.

Not being a man to have any doubts about his abilities, nor of his popularity with his peers, he had been surprised that his name had not been accepted uncontested, as had been the case in the last two contests. More surprising still was the nature of the opposition. A conspiracy of Europeans and Americans had put forward the name of one of the principle Russian bosses. This was later aggravated by the announcement that Riccardo's elder brother was also entering the fray. It looked as if these two were set to be his main rivals, and he seemed to be losing ground to both of them.

He thought he knew Giovanni pretty well, and was certain that he had no greater desire to stand now than he had when his father died. It would never occur to him that Giovanni had put his name forward now simply to prevent his own election, so it must be an attempt to stave off the Russian threat.

Joe was a small, wiry man with spikey light brown hair and a large slightly hooked nose, giving him a somewhat eagle-like appearance. He was filled to the very brim with pent-up energy, which caused his body to be constantly on the move, as were his lips - for he talked ten to the dozen. All his sentences were joined up, without any breaks, which tended to end as monologues rather than conversations. Most of them contained at least one swearword and if he had ever heard of political correctness, he did not believe that it applied to him.

Provided his plane from Europe was on time, Giovanni would be calling shortly, and he was gearing himself up for a showdown.

He was born nearly forty years earlier in Detroit to second-generation American parents. He was a late arrival as his father, who had worked all his life on a variety of General Motors assembly lines, would not countenance having children without proper funding. He was a strict and sober father, not through any religious convictions, but by the example and instruction of his own father who had been steeped in austerity and hard work.

No additions were made to the family and early life was tough for little Joe. He rebelled violently against his father's austerity when he reached his teenage years, skipping school and starting on a life of petty crime with an unsavoury gang of lifelong delinquents. His parents could neither understand nor tolerate it and reacted with anger and violence. That alienated Joe still further and kicked off the classic downward spiral which ended with Joe storming out of the family home for ever. From that moment on, he had neither seen nor communicated with his parents in any way.

By the time he was eighteen, he had moved to Chicago and graduated from minor delinquency to more organised criminality. Although known to the police he had never been successfully prosecuted, and he became convinced by the easy pickings that working for a living was a game for mugs only. He soaked up all the tricks of the trade like a sponge and was willing to take on anything that was entrusted to him. This made him very popular with his bosses and he rapidly rose through the ranks to the point where the borders between criminality and a more traditional idea of work became blurred. He found himself behind a desk organising a mixture of legitimate businesses and criminal operations.

Now, approaching his fortieth birthday, he was at the height of his powers. Yet he felt that something was missing. He had been involved in a string of relationships, a couple of which had lasted for more than a year, but they had all floundered on the rocks strewn by the nature of his occupation, and in particular by the very long hours involved. Although he was very rarely alone, he frequently felt lonely.

"Ciao Joe" Giovanni greeted him in the manner he always did. They walked round the corner to the little Italian restaurant Joe had booked for lunch.

They had always tolerated each other, but that was the limit of their relationship. Giovanni appreciated Joe's tireless and sometimes inspired work but disliked nearly everything about his looks, his bad language, his irascible manner and the crazy schemes he came up with every so often. In turn, Joe was somewhat in awe of Giovanni's legendry deeds and also his family connections. Both spiritually and culturally they had little in common, and their conversations were invariably limited to business matters.

"Hey, Giovanni. Come sta?" Joe asked, challenging Giovanni's knowledge of Italian and setting out a hostile tone for the meeting. "What the fuck have you been up to in Europe?"

"Oh, just had a bit of business in Italy. Nothing you need to worry about. I'm sure you'll be happy with it."

"Ah. What's all this, you wily old bugger?"

"Well. It concerns this Russian fella, Rubeliev..."

Becker was unable to contain himself and cut in immediately, "Yeah. It don't make no fucking sense, do it? And it's my opinion we're just making it easier for him - splitting the vote over here. That don't make no sense to me neither." Joe paused very briefly - as long as he ever paused between thoughts. "Listen, why the hell are you standing anyway? You don't want the fucking job. You didn't want it when yer old man died, and you don't want it now. So what the fuck are you...?"

"For Christ's sake, just shut up and listen for a change, Joe" Giovanni was already irritated, but trying to keep his calm. "We've been through all this. You remember we spoke at length on the phone - only last week, I think it was."

Becker managed to refrain from filling a short pause so Giovanni continued, "I don't know if you were serious or whether it was just some throwaway remark, but it was you who suggested we should take the Ruskie out of the frame. You remember?"

He paused briefly as Joe simply stared at him and then continued, "Well, I talked it over with Carl, and in the end, we came to the same conclusion. It seems to be the only solution left to us. We've been forced into a dark corner." He held his hand up as Becker made as if to break in again

"But we've got to be very careful, Joe. The timing will point the finger directly at us - you and me. I don't like it one bit, but I just can't see another way."

Becker's eyes rounded and widened in surprise, making him look even more like a bird of prey. This news was entirely unexpected. He was aware that some of his schemes were considered eccentric, but this was something else. He could not remember making the suggestion although it has entered his mind on several occasions. But it surprised him that Giovanni seemed to have accepted it as a real possibility.

"So what have you done, Giovanni? Who've you got for the job?" Joe asked excitedly.

"You don't know him, Joe. We can't use one of our own men - that's quite clear. So Carl and I have contracted a Limey - one I've used before. He's very reliable. The job couldn't be in better hands." He reassured Joe, but then added, "It won't be easy though."

"What's all this about you and Carl Fossen?" demanded Becker, "I heard he was acting as your running mate. But who's running who? That's what I'd fucking well like to know. He's a piece of shit, for Chris' sake."

Harry couldn't disagree with this last sentiment, but he was not about to enter into a dialogue with Becker about his relationship with Fossen.

"None of your business, Bob," Harry said quietly, but firmly. "He's got loads of useful contacts for a start."

Joe was so pleased with this news of the intended assassination that did not press his point further. But he was not about to let Giovanni off the hook about his candidacy without a fight. "That'll leave just the two of us then," he said. "Why don't you back off? You don't want the fucking job. Leave it to the next generation."

"I guess you don't understand, Joe. It's a family thing. When Pa died, Riccardo was there to take over. Now, there's no one but me. I simply gotta give it a shot."

"But what if the contract fails? Splitting our vote will just let this fucking Ruskie in," Joe cried.

"Perhaps. It's possible, Joe. As I say, hitting this guy won't be easy, and there ain't much time. It could well fail. But if you're that worried, you could always stand down yourself. Eh, Joe?"

"No way, man. Why the fuck should I?" exploded Joe.

Giovanni simply shrugged, which seemed to anger Joe still further. The deadlock was complete and, after a couple more skirmishes, Giovanni excused himself. He had delivered his news and had a plane to catch.

Chapter 8

Tatyana was still asleep as Harry swiftly turned off the alarm. He managed to shave and dress without waking her, then bent over to kiss her. They had said their goodbyes the night before and he saw no reason to wake her now. He looked at the face he loved so dearly for some time and listened to her slow breathing. Then he gave her one last kiss and turned to go.

"Harry!" she called gently, with a waking tremor. He turned back and they kissed once more. "Be ever so careful, darling. And phone me often".

"I will. Back to sleep," he suggested, and then, "Bye, darling" as he picked up the case he had packed the night before and closed the door quietly behind him.

As usual, he left their ageing Audi for Tatyana to use whilst he was away. The journey by train was easy enough but somewhat unpredictable, so he had allowed plenty of time. Besides, he wanted to get himself a good breakfast. The food on the plane was likely to be inedible.

In the event, he was late getting to the Boarding Gate and was one of the last to take his seat on the plane. The lady in the window seat beside him was deeply immersed in The Telegraph and didn't look up as he eased himself into his chair and buckled his seatbelt. He happily took the hint that she wasn't the conversational type, and settled back for take-off.

It was only after the plane had begun to level off, and the pilot had switched off the seatbelt sign that she suddenly put down her paper. She turned to Harry with a huge smile on her face and said shrilly, "Surprise!"

He was indeed so surprised that all he could blurt out was her name, "T-Tania," and then, "What the hell..."

She took his arm and leaned toward him to hug him. A hundred thoughts flashed through his mind. He could kick up a fuss and put her on the next plane home as soon as they arrived. Or, he could accept what was probably inevitable now. He would perhaps be able to balance his fears for her safety with the possible advantages she had cited. With her in tow, he would probably be more cautious himself. He would certainly benefit hugely from her fluent Russian. And, of course, he would enjoy her company.

"How the hell did you manage to get that seat?"

"Influence," she smiled and then added, "I was lucky. It was a man at the check-in desk. I just batted my eyes a little and explained that I wanted to surprise my husband."

"Well, you certainly did that," and then, after a short pause, "OK. You win" he announced with a sigh, but also with a grin, and went on to accept her hug more enthusiastically.

Tatyana had not had time to get anything to eat and managed to tackle the breakfast they were served. Even though he had missed his airport breakfast, Harry happily passed on that, but he did have a couple of gin and tonics - early in the day perhaps, but something of a tradition for him when flying. He began to relax, and they arrived at Moscow's Domodedovo airport in good spirits, only dampened somewhat by the uneventful but tedious immigration formalities. Once through customs, they picked up the nondescript VW Golf that Harry had reserved. Fossen's dossier had included instructions to ensure that the rental car was equipped with a good navigation system, capable of directly entering GPS locations, and the hire company had thoughtfully set it to operate in English.

The airport was some distance from Moscow, but within half an hour the satnav was threading them through the dense Moscow traffic towards their hotel on the Rublevo-Uspenskoe Highway. The rush hour was beginning to die away now and this road sparkled in the late afternoon sun. In sharp contrast to the miles of densely packed apartment buildings they had already passed, it was tree-lined with neat grass verges, marred only by large hoardings advertising everything conceivable that could be desired by the rich and famous.

The Barvikha hotel was almost new and catered principally for businessmen with sturdy expense accounts. Giovanni's pockets were deep and the job he had been given deserved a degree of comfort, Harry thought. This hotel and spa offered it in considerable measure, and the room they entered was large and decorated principally in natural woods. It had a king-size bed and a separate sitting area which in turn led to a private balcony. As Harry tipped the liveried porter, Tatyana threw herself onto the bed and looked around the room. They would certainly be comfortable here, she thought.

Although there were many good restaurants in the area, the journey had taken its toll and, after a couple of drinks at the Bar, they headed for the hotel restaurant where they each enjoyed a good steak accompanied by a Bordeaux that was as ordinary as it was expensive. Back in their room, Harry idly clicked through the satellite television channels settling finally on some news from CNN.

The following morning, they planned their day. In the old Soviet days, foreigners in particular were under constant surveillance and hotel rooms were regularly bugged. Harry considered it most unlikely nowadays but Tatyana, who had been brought up under a similar regime, still voiced her suspicions. She turned the CNN News back on and insisted that they made their plans in hushed tones. Harry smiled at her little eccentricity but was happy to humour her.

It had become clear from Fossen's files that the main obstacle, even before any kill plan could be devised, would be to find a way of getting close access to Rubeliev. The first step would have to be thorough reconnoitres of both his home and the factory, and this morning they decided to tackle the latter.

The Wykobka factory was located at the corner of an industrial estate about twenty minutes' drive away. The main factory entrance was on the side street, and Harry drove straight past it taking in the surroundings that resembled any industrial park anywhere in the world. As he turned the car around towards the rear of the estate, he made a note on a slip of paper of the name proudly emblazoned in large letters on one of the buildings. He then returned and parked opposite, but well short of the Wykobka entrance, where he hoped it would be concealed amongst the other cars and vans that littered both sides of the road.

Like most others on the estate, the Wykobka site was surrounded by a high block wall and the entrance was barred by a single pole barrier. It was guarded by two armed security guards in dark blue military-style uniforms, who popped out from a small office each time a car pulled in, examined badges and raised the barrier. These were probably employees arriving for work at this time of day, thought Harry.

After about ten minutes, a car drew up whose occupant was not recognised, or at least did not have the necessary badge. He was waved to a holding parking bay where he got out and was ushered into the office where they could see a telephone call being made. Once satisfied that the visitor was expected, the barrier was raised and he was shown through. Harry felt he had seen enough. He had never really expected this to be a viable route to his target.

"I don't think you'll have much joy here, darling." Tatyana seemed to agree.

Harry grunted broodingly and went to start the car. As he did so, one of the guards stepped out of the office and started walking purposely towards them. "Damn!" exclaimed Harry.

He passed the piece of paper to Tatyana. "You speak to him. Ask him where these people are," he said. He took the map from her lap and started to study it closely. She lowered her window and called to the man as he approached, "Excuse me! We're not sure we're in the right place." She showed him the paper and asked. "Do you know where this company is?"

The man looked at the name and pointed down the road. "Almost to the end, on the right. It's clearly marked," he said shortly and started to walk away. "Thank you!" she shouted after him. He raised a hand but kept walking. The road had been designed to accommodate large vehicles, and Harry was able to turn again in one. There did not appear to be any other way out of the estate, so they parked out of sight for a quarter of an hour before leaving. Whilst they waited, Harry dug out the sketchy plan from Fossen's dossier as he had recalled that there was a second entrance. It was located on the main road, and it seemed they had already passed it upon entering the estate without noticing it.

Harry had no desire to be spotted again, so decided it would be too risky to stop. He swung round and took a camera out of the holdall lying on the back seat. "Here, Tania. Take a couple of shots of the other entrance as we pass. I don't want to stop again." She nodded and started making a couple of adjustments to the camera settings as Harry re-started the engine and moved off.

As they passed the entrance, even from the opposite side of the main road, it was clearly unlikely to be of much use to them. Two high steel gates filled the entrance flush with the dark brown brick elevation. They could make out nothing else and continued back to the hotel.

Harry smiled as Tatyana turned the TV back on before quietly questioning, "On to the house, darling?"

"I suppose so," he replied. "Let's just have a look at the photos before we do." He picked up the camera and they sat down together on the sofa. She had managed to take several shots of the main road entrance. Zooming in, Harry could just make out a small intercom just to the left of the door, but that was all.

Rubeliev's house was identified on a map prepared by Fossen's men and turned out to be several miles to the east of their hotel on a road off the main highway. The traffic was somewhat less frenetic here and Harry was able to drive past the house fairly slowly.

It was a large site, some couple of hundred yards or so wide, and was guarded by eight foot high solid green metal fencing, topped by razor wire. Towards the centre and set back from the main perimeter, was a pair of high steel gates matching the fencing. There was no intercom to announce visitors since the gates were permanently manned by two men in plain clothes, no doubt well armed, who occupied a small office to the right hand side of the setback. This also housed a bank of monitors from the security cameras which could be seen over the entrance gates and at intervals along the whole length of the fence. The house itself was large and seemed to be roughly in the centre of the site, but only the top floor was visible from the street. Again, it was just as he had feared, thought Harry.

Opposite the site was a small collection of commercial buildings – a café, a few shops, some offices and a restaurant whose garish advertising insisted that they served the best, but still the cheapest, lunches in the district. Harry parked in a small area of rough ground that served as a car park and, with nobody around, Tatyana took some photos of the Rubeliev site opposite. They got out of the car, crossed the road and walked nonchalantly along the pavement chatting to each other, but also examining the fence close-up in the hope of spotting some vulnerability. Finding none, they re-crossed the road back to the shops.

By now it was coming up to lunchtime and, passing up on the cheapest lunch around, they decided on a sandwich in the café. As they entered, the place was buzzing with building workers all talking loudly as they tucked into a variety of rather unappetising looking breakfast dishes, but they did manage to find a table by the window. The general babble died down and eyes turned to follow Tatyana as she made her way to the counter to place their order. She was used to this sort of attention, of course, and returned to their table with a broad smile on her face.

Meanwhile, Harry used this diversion to study the location from a wider viewpoint. The plot to the right of Rubeliev's house was a building site. It was surrounded by rough wooden shuttering and, towards the right hand boundary, high wooden double doors lay wide open. A large ready-mix concrete vehicle was being ushered in by a security guard. During the time they ate, they saw a couple more lorries arrive and then watched the workmen gradually saunter out of the café, cross the road and back into the site.

Harry had spotted some notices attached to the hoarding beside the open gates of the building site, and they crossed the road once again to read them. There were several closely printed laminated sheets which Tatyana explained were Planning and Building Notices.

Beside them were a couple of flyers by Property Agents, complete with an Architect's artistic impression of the completed building.

As Harry bent to study these, a tall gaunt man passed by and turned to look at them through small beady eyes set in a long pale face that was badly pockmarked. Harry was alarmed to realise that he knew the man, or had met him, or maybe just seen him somewhere - he could not remember where.

He smiled politely, as one does when meeting someone recognised but not remembered. Pock-man failed to smile back but looked intently at both of them in turn. Harry felt he could almost hear the click, click, click of a camera burst as the man tucked away images of them both in his mind. It all happened very quickly and he was past them in a moment. He then crossed the road to a parked car, and Harry noticed him glance back at them once more as he closed the door and slowly drove away.

Harry was disquieted by the incident. Where had he seen the man before? Possibly on the journey, but more probably at the hotel, he thought. The restaurant had been crowded on the previous evening and they had seen many new faces. It would come to him if he put it out of his mind for a while, and he turned back to jotting down names and details of the selling Agents. He noted too that a large padlock swung from one of the open doors, clearly used to secure the site when the last of the workmen left for the day.

As they drove back to the hotel, they debriefed themselves on the morning's findings. They both agreed that the factory site was unlikely to offer many possibilities. Harry had originally thought that Rubeliev's journey to and from work might prove the best chance, but he was now inclined to dismiss this too, as there was much more traffic than he had imagined, particularly at the times Rubeliev travelled. He knew that time was not on his side and, unless he could catch his prey somewhere in the open, it just left the Rubeliev house itself.

Chapter 9

The discovery of the building site had given Harry the germ of an idea that he was determined to pursue. If he could gain access to it at a time after building work had finished, it may yield a clear sight for a shot at Rubeliev in his house or garden. The strategy would much depend on the strength of after-hours security, but it seemed to be the best opportunity so far.

Back in the hotel, Tatyana went off to the Spa for a session on the exercise machines - something she did several times a week at her fitness club at home. Harry joined her later and they swam lengths of the pool together, this being Harry's favourite means of keeping fit. He simply could not face the boredom of weights or static cycling machines.

That evening they ate out at a nearby Italian restaurant. Harry was rather subdued throughout the meal as his mind kept returning to the plan that was beginning to take shape, the hardware that would be needed and a timetable of events. For a start, any shot he might get of his target would probably be at quite a distance, so something much more than a revolver would be required. Harry had not yet decrypted the contact details for the armourer, so he had no idea how far he would have to go for any necessary weapons. He would have to plan very carefully all the items he was likely to need.

Back in their room, he dug out the armourer's details from Fossen's dossier. When they had parted, Fossen had verbally given him the necessary decryption key, with the sobering information that it would die with him or after four weeks, whichever happened earlier. He began to decrypt the text onto a sheet of hotel notepaper. When he had finished, it read simply "Vulcan. Are you open for business on Thursday next?" and "No, but I am open today" followed by a landline telephone number. Vulcan was presumably the armourer's moniker, the remainder being simple question-and-answer passphrases for use to verify an introduction. There was no address or other information. He decided to leave the telephone call until the morning.

Harry was wakened early the next day by the sun streaming through the curtains. With Tatyana still asleep, he continued to think through his plan. His lack of fluency in the language meant there was little chance of conning his way into the site during construction hours. On the other hand, even with a night sight, he felt it was unlikely that he would be able to get a successful shot after dark. It would be necessary then to gain entry during the very early hours of the morning, and to await signs of movement in the Rubeliev household. Fossen's dossier had indicated that Rubeliev tried to lead a normal family life, but Harry did not doubt that the two security guards they had seen at the gate were unlikely to be alone. There would almost certainly be more inside the house itself.

And the thought of the family itself, including the two young boys, suddenly jerked his conscience and reminded him of his army days in the Iraq War. He had witnessed several distressing scenes involving children, and he must be sure to make certain there was no collateral damage on this job. If he was to accomplish his task, it was bad enough that the children would lose their father.

The only day of the week that he could be sure that there would be no construction work was a Sunday. Russian workers normally worked a five day week, but he knew Saturday was also worked by many trades, and he had to be certain that there would be no one on the site. As it was, he would still have to investigate the possibility of there being a round-the-clock security guard on site. Harry looked at his watch instinctively. Today was Wednesday, and there was much to do before Sunday next.

For a start, he would have to decide on a method of entry. He would examine the hoarding more closely for any possible weakness, but he did not hold up much hope of this. He had no illusions about his ability to pick the lock, and the chunkiness of the padlock suggested considerable strength. He also had to think of his exit. If he was successful, it was likely that the alarm would be raised very quickly and he would be hard-pressed to get out and away. By far the best solution would be to somehow to obtain a copy of the padlock key. Whatever type it turned out to be, Harry felt sure that the armourer would be able to make a copy if only he was able to take a mould. He would need a good deal of luck, he realised, as he began to write out a short list of items he would need.

Tatyana was still asleep, but he managed to rouse her with a series of lingering kisses starting with her forehead, down her nose and on to her mouth. Her tired arms emerged wearily from below the sheets and wound around Harry's neck forcing him further into her now open lips. After a few seconds, he pulled himself away saying, "Enough, my darling. Up you get. Work to be done..."

Over breakfast, Harry outlined his plan and timetable for the day. The morning would be spent on separate tasks. He had some purchases to make and would take the car to the retail park at the beginning of the Rublevo-Uspenskoe Highway. Tatyana was to visit the nearer of the two selling agents which was within a short walking distance of the hotel, obtain as much information on the property as possible, and then to make an appointment for them to visit the site, preferably that afternoon or evening. It was a long shot, but he might be able to spot the padlock key perhaps hanging on the hoarding or maybe in a site office. If only he could get possession of it for five minutes to himself.

They had arranged to meet up and compare notes over lunch at the hotel, but Tatyana was neither in the Bistro nor their room when Harry returned from the Auchan store at Rublevo. He delved into his plastic shopping bag and took out a small but sturdy metal box containing half a dozen white chalks, which he took out and placed on the sideboard. Next out of the bag were several tubes of children's red Plasticine clay which he emptied into his hand and kneaded into a soft round ball. He placed this in the tin and worked it around until it was totally filled to its rims. He scraped away the excess with his penknife and smoothed the surface flat. He then closed the lid and put it in his pocket, along with his other purchases – one round and one flat metal file, and a couple of screwdrivers.

Tatyana returned shortly afterwards and, having showered in the fitness centre was ready for lunch. It would have to be fairly quick, she said, as the only appointment they could give her today was at two thirty.

Tatyana had arranged to meet the agent in the same small car park opposite the site. They arrived and parked on time but there were no other cars. They remained inside the car, wishing to remain out of sight for as long as possible. It was more than ten minutes before a small sports car pulled in with a screech of brakes, and a young man bounced out. Typical of Property Agents the world over, he was a handsome lad. Long blond hair flowed around a wide sun-tanned, but slightly angular, face enlivened by wide dark eyes. He shook hands with only a slight smile and wasted little time on a lame apology for his lateness. Almost ignoring Harry, he started to push Tatyana over the busy road. She explained to him that her husband did not speak or understand any Russian, and he was clearly more than happy to give her all his attention as they entered the site.

As they passed through the gates, Harry was amazed to spot the key still resting in the padlock as it hung open. It may be convenient for the builders perhaps, but how very lazy he thought, and a great piece of luck for him.

By this time, Tatyana had worked her usual charms, and the poor Agent was madly in love with her, laughing and joking as they entered the shell of the house. Harry caught up with them briefly and said to

Tatyana, "I've forgotten the camera. I'll just nip back to the car and get it. OK?" The Agent raised no objection.

Most of the workmen were busy banging, sawing or laying blocks inside the house, but one man was in the front tending a cement mixer. Harry calculated that the angle was such that he was unlikely to see him at the gate, but timed his exit to coincide with the man emptying a load into his barrow. He was able to pull the key very easily from the padlock as he passed and crossed the road to the car. Opening the box of Plasticine, he very carefully made impressions of both sides of the key, and finally one of the end of the barrel. He closed the lid, placed it in the glove box, got out the camera and crossed the road again. Nobody was around as he replaced the key in the padlock.

Pleased with the operation, he had just started to take a few photos when Tatyana called from one of the windows, "Harry. Sergei says you shouldn't be taking photos." Harry shouted back, "Oh! Tell him sorry". He put the lens hood back on, slung the camera around his neck and went into the house to join them. Sergei clearly doesn't understand much English, Harry thought.

After a quick look around the ground floor, he left the two of them looking through a brochure and went up to the first. This was going to be a big house and Harry smiled at the thought that Russian Agents advertise such buildings as cottages. He moved over to a window that overlooked the Rubeliev house and was pleased with what he saw.

The security fence continued around the entire perimeter of the site and appeared to consist of the same measures of high security. Some boundary trees had been planted but were too immature to block the view entirely. Like the house they were in, it was large and of three storeys. At the front, a cobbled drive surrounded a circle of lawn and pond whose centrepiece was a statue consisting of a triplet of Nymphs frolicking in the water that splashed around them from a fountain. Surrounded by more grass and some flowerbeds, a single-storey garage block stood between the house and a tree-lined security fence.

Harry moved to another window further to the back of the house, where he could get a better view of the neighbouring garden. A paved terrace decked out with a variety of garden furniture led down to a good size swimming pool. The trees here seemed to be somewhat larger, but there were still numerous gaps. Harry decided immediately that this would be where he would take up his position.

He looked around him. The building was still very much a block and concrete shell, and much of the first floor was stacked with building materials of all kinds. On trestle tables were piles of insulation and plasterboard ready to line the walls, with sacks of plaster in one corner. Harry took the stairs up to the second floor where he found that the views offered no particular advantage. It was much more open here, as the workers were still constructing the internal walls.

Harry joined the others outside the building where he found them pouring over some rather large and unwieldy plans. The agent looked up as he arrived, and he tapped the camera and mouthed, "Sorry" which Sergei acknowledged with a short smile and a nod of the head, then went back to talking with Tatyana. When they had finished their discussions, Tatyana looked up at Harry.

"Sergei wants to know if you have any questions before he goes. He has another appointment."

"I don't think so," Harry replied. "We know where to contact him if I do think of anything."

Back in the car park, they both thanked and shook hands with Sergei, who was still clearly finding it difficult to take his eyes off Tatyana - even as he sped off.

Back in the hotel, Harry decided it was time to call the armourer and dug out the data he had decrypted. He had no idea how secure landline telephones were in Russia, particularly those from a hotel, so he was somewhat apprehensive as to how much he would be able to say. He telephoned the specified number and almost immediately a man answered with a simple, "Da". Harry spoke the introductory sentence and, after a long pause, got the correct reply in heavily accented English.

"Hello, Vulcan." Harry opened. "Do you speak English?"

"A little. Enough. But not speak on telephone. When do you come?"

"Tomorrow... if possible"

"You are in Moscow?"

"Yes."

"Take M2 motorway south - about one hour and half. I expect you about ten in the morning. Do you have paper and pen?"

"Yes," Harry confirmed.

"Write this carefully." He then proceeded to slowly dictate a series of alphanumeric characters.

"Please read to me". Harry complied and it was agreed as correct.

"If you decode, that will give GPS directions to follow. Look for green door. There is a bell. Do svidaniya." Vulcan rang off. That was it. No opportunity to find out where he was going or have any discussion of his needs.

Harry pulled over more hotel notepaper and began to carefully decrypt the message. When he had finished it read simply, "N 54.1148, E 37.3741."

Chapter 10

The following morning it was decided that Harry would travel alone to see the armourer - "boys' stuff" as Tatyana had dismissed it. Once he had entered the GPS address into the navigation system, it picked his way for him to the M2 travelling south. After an hour or so he passed the city of Tula, which he knew was renowned for arms manufacturing of all descriptions. At the next major junction, he turned off to the right where it became more and more uninhabited until he eventually arrived at the designated location. He followed a track that led off to a large building where, sure enough, he spotted a dark green door.

After a short delay, the bell was answered by a short, stubby man dressed in blue overalls. He looked up at Harry and there was a moment's silence until Harry suddenly realised that an introduction was required.

"I was wondering," he started, "are you open for business on Thursday next?"

The man replied with a smile, "No, but we are open today. Please come in."

Once inside, he offered his hand with "I am Vulcan". A receding knot of wispy pale brown hair circled a round pasty face sporting large brown eyes and a wide mouth with generous over-full lips. They shook hands, but Harry did not offer his name. With some desultory conversation about the good weather and the journey, he was led through a maze of corridors and rooms until they finally reached a large workshop full of machinery. A young man was working one of the machines in the far corner, but he was the only other person in the room. To the left as they entered was an office area with a desk beside a couple of chairs and some cabinets. Vulcan moved behind the desk and waved Harry to a chair.

As he sat down, Vulcan said quietly, "I have done work for Giovanni, and met him one time. He is nice man. Yes?"

He did not seem to expect a reply and went on immediately, "He says for me to do whatever I can to help you. Now! What you want?"

Harry thought for a few seconds, then decided that he should give no details whatsoever of his mission, nor the reasons for his particular requirements. He was sure that Vulcan would not wish to know and, because of the time it might take, he decided to start with the key. He got out the box with the Plasticine mould from his pocket and placed it on the table in front of Vulcan saying, "I took this mould from a padlock key. Will you be able to make a decent copy from it and, if so, how long will it take?"

Vulcan picked up the tin and studied the contents carefully under a bright desk light. "Is good," he pronounced eventually, and continued, "But... three different tasks to make key." He held out three fingers and thought some more. "If I start Valerie now," he hesitated, thinking, then, "maybe... tomorrow evening."

"That'll be fine," Harry said. "I'll pick it up on Saturday morning – at the same time. OK?" Vulcan shrugged and nodded his head in agreement.

"I will need a sniper's rifle." Vulcan had gone a bit quiet but was visibly more excited by this request.

"Good. What range?" Vulcan asked.

For some reason, Harry had not expected this and he took a moment or two to visualise the scene. He decided to err on the generous side and replied, "Between a hundred and two hundred yards."

"No problem," Vulcan said, and then asked another question. "What have you used before? Do you have favourite?"

Harry had to think again. Then he said, "I've used quite a few in my time, the British RPA Rangemaster, an L42 Enfield, an XM2010..."

"I can get an XM2010," said Vulcan. "But it will take a few days. If you need quickly, I have good local models. I can say is good a VSS "Vintorez". You know it?" He walked over to a large heavy steel cabinet, unlocked it and took out a case that looked rather like a briefcase, but with a rounded top. He carried it over to the desk, opened the lid and assembled the five sections of the rifle in less than ten seconds.

"All ready." He swept his hands open as if he had just performed a trick of magic. "Has noise suppressor and telescopic sight all included." He looked up at Harry for a sign of approval. Harry was indeed impressed and gave him a nod. Vulcan took out one of the two magazines that were in the case and went back to the cupboard, where he carefully pushed in five bullets. "Come. You try it." He picked up the rifle and beckoned with it for Harry to follow him.

They left the building and walked for a hundred yards or so to an area well hidden from the road by trees. There was a small hut and a short length of brick wall and, in the distance, Harry could see a series of grass-covered mounds, all fairly overgrown. It seemed that Vulcan had made himself a mini firing range. He unlocked the hut and took out a small target which he took to the second of the mounds and fixed it to a wooden post. When he returned, he tapped the rifle and said, "Two hundred. Is good up to four hundred yards. Lethal."

Vulcan punched the magazine into the rifle and handed it to Harry. "Five shots," he said.

Harry took the rifle and walked over to the wall, then stopped and looked at Vulcan to see whether he should use it as a rest. Vulcan smiled, pursed his lips and opened his hands as if to say, "OK. Use it if you must". Harry moved away from the wall and shot five times at the target. The sound suppressing system was impressive and, looking though the telescopic sight, he saw a neat tight grouping. By the time he came to put the gun down, Vulcan was on his way to retrieve the target.

Back inside the workshop, they agreed that no adjustments would be needed for the intended range. Vulcan went through the routines for disassembly and reassembly and got Harry to practice them a couple of times before packing it away again in the briefcase. Separately, he handed Harry a magazine with 20 cartridges loaded. "More than enough – hopefully," Harry said.

"One last thing; I need a hand gun - something lethal at close range, quiet and small enough to conceal on my body easily. Any suggestions?"

Vulcan did not hesitate but marched once more to the cabinet and took out a small handgun. He started to walk back towards Harry but then turned back and picked up a holster. With a wide smile, he looked very satisfied as he returned to Harry and said, "Something very special for you - a PSS Noiseless pistol. Just a small click - noise suppressor not needed."

"I've read of them," said Harry. "They use special ammunition don't they?"

"Yes. SP-4 cartridge - made here in Tula." Vulcan said somewhat triumphantly. "Has a... er... thing inside that traps gasses when gun is fired. They are difficult to get, even here, and expensive - but very good for you I think"

"OK," Harry smiled. "That completes my list. Thank you."

Vulcan went through the safety and other features of the pistol and fitted Harry with the shoulder holster. It felt somewhat bigger than others he'd worn but was inconspicuous enough when he put his jacket on. Vulcan pulled out the magazine and walked to the cabinet once more. "Ten rounds OK?" As Harry nodded, he loaded the magazine and handed it back to him.

The two men shook hands, and it was agreed that Harry would pick up all three items on Saturday morning. He did not want them in his possession any longer than was necessary.

The drive back to the hotel was uneventful and he recounted the morning's events to Tatyana over a late lunch. With a firm plan and timetable now in place, Harry had some nagging concerns that he needed to address urgently. For a start, he was acutely conscious that he had not yet established that Rubeliev would actually be in the house on Sunday morning. Nor had he given much thought as to how this could be done without compromising his security and anonymity.

As he voiced these concerns, Tatyana said nothing but moved to the desk and pulled out the telephone directory. She picked up the receiver, punched in a number and waited, giving Harry a mischievous wink.

Suddenly, she said in a poor form of Russian, "Hello, yes. Could I please speak to Mr Victor Rubeliev?" Harry stared at her, wide-eyed and moved towards her. She held up a hand for him to stop.

After pausing for a reply, she said, "I am speaking for Mr Riccardo Pollini."

After another, longer pause, "No. I have to give him the message personally."

There was another long pause before she started in a very passable southern American drawl, "Hello. Victor Rubeliev?"

Satisfied with his reply, she continued, "I have a message from Riccardo Pollini. He is undergoing some medical treatment at this time, and can't speak with you right now. I do hope you understand."

But she got a more positive response as she continued, "He does wish to speak with you and hopes to be better at the weekend - perhaps Sunday. Will you be there in Moscow if he puts through a call?"

"Good. I'll let him know. Thank you. Bye." She put her finger down quickly on the button to cut the line, then replaced the receiver gently into the cradle and turned to Harry with another smile. "All done. He'll be there."

Harry kissed her but she'd now managed to raise more questions than she'd answered. What if their line was bugged? Wouldn't they check the authenticity of the call? However, he wasn't about to burst the little bubble of pride she felt in her effort. And the security arrangements within the building were of greater concern, and he was uncertain how he could discover any more details.

On Friday they had nothing very constructive to achieve, so Tatyana decided to do some shopping in central Moscow. They already had some of Giovanni's money in the bank and she felt it deserved a serious assault. She did not want Harry with her as he always cramped her style during retail expeditions. He could make himself useful, she said, by driving her to a railway station since she had no wish to tangle with Moscow's traffic. She would phone when she needed to be picked up. Harry was relaxed about this as he knew that she was well acquainted with Moscow's city centre, and she certainly deserved some recreation time.

As he returned from dropping her off at the Barvikha station, about two miles away, he decided to have one more look at the site. He would be entering the dark and wanted to implant a clear picture in his mind. He drove past it and continued for about half a mile along the side road, which was lined on both sides with similar large houses. He turned and drove back past the site one last time. The wooden doors were open, the key once again in the dangling lock, and inside was a large lorry delivering a load of materials.

Tatyana did not surface until late in the afternoon. As Harry drove her back from the station with all her purchases, Tatyana was bubbling over with excitement. The moment they were back in their room, she sat Harry down and proceeded to give him a private fashion show of all the underwear, dresses, shoes and other bit and pieces she had bought. Her face was highly coloured with the thrill of it all, and her blond curls danced as she bobbed and twirled. Harry was genuinely entranced and applauded each item, but found it increasingly difficult to contain himself. Finally, as she was exhibiting some bits of skimpy underwear, he could bear it no longer. He leapt up, grabbed her and threw her on the bed where they spent the next twenty minutes making rough and tender love alternately. Finally, she said "You've got to let me go shopping more often." They both laughed, but the fashion show was over.

In the morning, Harry left for Tula and the armourer. Vulcan introduced him to his assistant, who had done the majority of the work on the padlock key and who turned out to be his son. With some pride, they showed him how snugly the key slipped into the Plasticine mould. Harry offered several due words of appreciation and pocketed the key. Next, he took off the loose jacket he had selected to wear and was fitted with the pistol in its holster. As he was handed the rifle in its case, he began to feel like Laurence Olivier's Henry V, preparing to do battle at Agincourt.

During the journey back, Harry had decided that he would chance leaving the rifle in the car. He would be using it in a few hours anyway and did not wish to be seen carrying the briefcase in and out of the hotel. He searched in vain for a suitable hiding place inside the car, so left it where it lay concealed in the boot.

There was little to do but relax for the rest of the day. Harry went onto the internet to discover the time the sun would be rising the following morning. He had to be on the site by 5.30 am at the latest and decided he would leave the hotel at least an hour earlier and set the alarm clock for twenty past four.

Sleep did not come easily that night as Harry's mind previewed the task that lay before him on the following day. They had laid the groundwork well, he thought, but there were still a number of outstanding concerns. For a start, would he recognise Rubeliev? He had only seen his face in photographs. And would his prey ever venture into the garden to present himself as a target? Vulcan's key had looked good in the mould, but would it open the padlock?

And he knew very little of the site security. Would any movement set off an alarm? Would the cameras merely record events or would they relay live images of him to a remote security firm? Was a watchman employed to be on site for the weekend? He was aware of many such unknowns, but what of Donald Rumsfeld's "unknown unknowns"? With little chance now of resolving these imponderables, he managed to fall into a deep sleep.

Chapter 11

Harry was awoken by the alarm, which also woke Tatyana. He had put out everything he would need the previous evening, so it was not long before he was ready to leave. But before he slipped out of the room, Tatyana gave him a lingering kiss and wished him luck. Then she turned over as if to sleep. She knew she wouldn't be able to do so, but she didn't want him worrying over her concerns.

In the entrance hall, the night clerk looked up from whatever he was reading under his desk and stood up as Harry passed. "Morning," said Harry as he left through the doors. The man sat down again and went back to his book. Harry briefly checked that the briefcase was still in the boot and then drove off.

He passed only one car on the short journey and was able to park quietly opposite the site, just off the road with the car facing in the direction of his escape. He remained in the car for a short time scanning the scene, but he could detect no movement or other eyes around. Silently, he slipped out with the briefcase and a plastic bag containing a couple of sandwiches and a Coke he had picked up the night before.

The key turned in the padlock like a dream, and he offered up a silent thanks to Vulcan Junior that he would have to make no adjustments. He poked up the lapels of his jacket but took no other steps to conceal his face as he closed the gates, taking the key out and leaving the padlock hanging half-closed. He put the key in his pocket and entered the house. No doubt, infrared cameras had already taken video of his entry, but he breathed a sigh of relief that no alarm had sounded.

Once on the first floor, Harry assembled the rifle, attached the magazine, and placed it on a pile of plasterboard sheets next to his chosen window opening. He was disappointed not to find a chair of any sort within the building but managed to get reasonably comfortable by nuzzling himself into a pile of bags of insulation material. The early morning chill made him glad Tatyana had insisted he should put a sweater on under his jacket. He had included a book in his comfort pack, but it was still much too dark to read. He started to munch through one of the sandwiches and settled down to a long wait for dawn and hopefully the emergence of his prey.

Harry was too excited to sleep easily and began to consider the surreal situation he was in. How could it be that a perfectly ordinary Englishman, such as he, could find himself sitting amongst a pile of sacks in the middle of the night in the shell of a building and in a foreign land, waiting to kill another human being - a man who he had never met? He pondered the sequence of life choices he had made that had steered him to this bizarre position.

He had left school with a good education and with perfectly reasonable grades in his exams, but he lacked a calling into any particular career. Nor had he wished to attend university, which caused much friction with his father who was very keen on the idea. He had not liked the thought of working in an office, preferring a more muscular, open-air occupation. Eventually, he decided that a career in the Army might suit him, and he managed to obtain a place at Sandhurst where he was commissioned as a Lieutenant a year later. The life did indeed suit him - the discipline and security, the camaraderie in the Mess, and in particular the opportunity to play a variety of sports, especially rugby where he played for the Army XV. And he very soon learned that the girls did love a good-looking man in an officer's uniform - a fact he took full advantage of.

Whilst he was enjoying all this, links with the family began to fall apart. He was conscientious enough and telephoned his parents every month, but he only went to see them a couple of times a year. Although they were always pleased to see him, eventually these visits did become a little strained.

Then, in 2003, Britain joined the United States in its invasion of Iraq and, as it did for many others, the world changed for Harry. He was almost immediately posted to the Basra Command, managing time for only a very short farewell visit home. Although it was good to get away from a British winter, the temperature in Basra very soon rose to unbearable levels, particularly when wearing heavy combat body armour. And he soon discovered that he had not been sufficiently prepared for the horrors of modern urban warfare, where the enemy merges with innocent civilians. He personally killed several people, at least one of whom he later thought was probably merely a bystander. And he became witness to many horrific deaths on both sides, among them to several children.

It was impossible not to become hardened to the very act of killing, but the fact that some were innocent civilians had a bruising effect on his attitude to his chosen career. It was helped to a large degree by a close friendship he developed with the commander of one of the other squads in his platoon. They became inseparable when not on duty and, after several months and a rather drunken session in the Mess, Bob had confided in Harry that his father was a professional assassin. He had always professed to be some sort of entrepreneur, a claim that Bob had never really challenged. However, he had frequently wondered how the family enjoyed such a good standard of living and, over his teenage years, he put together certain events and scraps of conversation which led him to suspect something of the truth. Perhaps his father realised this, because one evening he had laid it all out before Bob, who surprised himself by taking it in his stride.

Harry was surprised when his initial reaction was also one of amusement rather than shock. Indeed, it may have been the alcohol, but he burst out laughing when Bob told him the story. For a moment or two Bob was silent, looking puzzled, but then started to laugh too. The evening had ended with both of them rolling around in uncontrolled fits of laughter until they were firmly invited to leave the Mess.

Soon after this, Bob had taken a bullet in the leg and was repatriated back to England. Harry had seen out the rest of his tour of duty without any major mishap, and when he returned to England it was not long before he got in touch with Bob. He found him walking with a pronounced limp and, rather than accept a desk job, he had been invalided out of the Army. Life had become tough, and the jobs he had been offered bored him to tears after his service life. Eventually, he had thrown his lot in with his father who found himself needing a second pair of hands as he got older.

Their friendship picked up where it had left off, and they met regularly over the months that followed. One day, Bob called him and they arranged to meet. His father had died unexpectedly and left him with a couple of jobs which would be very difficult to complete on his own. He knew that Harry was no longer happy in the Army, and wondered if he would join him. He thought that they would make a great team. Harry firmly turned him down at first but had given it second thoughts when a financially enticing opportunity to resign his commission had arisen.

He spent several weeks scouring his conscience. Was he really to become an assassin? The concept was so far from the natural moralities that he was amazed to find himself even considering the proposal. And yet...

He found himself vacillating between revulsion and mild euphoria at the thought of going into action once again with his friend by his side. Eventually, he managed to suborn his conscience, for a while at least, and convince himself that, if not within the law, at least they would be acting on the side of the righteous. Their targets would be far removed from the ordinary civilians he had encountered in Iraq. They would be villains of one sort or another, which society would not greatly miss.

And so, he did join Bob and they did indeed make a good team until Bob was killed in the Moscow raid. Left on his own, Harry had no stomach to continue and had happily agreed with his new wife that the venture was over.

But now he felt a void in his stomach as the doubts returned. He knew nothing of the quarry for which he was now waiting. He certainly had a wife and children. Why should he deprive them? Should he disengage now – simply walk away?

But again he steeled himself. Nothing had changed, he decided. Rubeliev must be an arch-villain – a hard, probably vicious man. And with his mind thus settled, he managed to fall asleep once more, cradled within the unyielding bags.

The sun streaming through the skeleton windows woke him with a start. He shivered as he rubbed the sleep from his eyes and patted his cheeks to get some circulation to his brain. Stretching out the stiffness from his joints, he crossed to the window and watched for some signs of movement. He looked at his watch. It was just coming up to eight o'clock, and on this Sunday morning, everything seemed as quiet as a tomb. How very ironic, Harry thought.

He finished his snack and stuffed the plastic bag into his pocket. After checking that the rifle was completely ready to fire, he stood to one side of the window and awaited some signs of activity.

He did not have to wait long. After less than ten minutes, he spotted a slight movement at the french doors that led out onto the terrace. He grabbed the rifle and went back to the window. His viewpoint was directly in line with the rear wall and it seemed with the naked eye that something was breaking the vertical plane of the door.

He raised the rifle and peered through the telescopic sight. Sure enough, he could see that a person was standing in the doorway looking out onto the garden. He could see the nose and sometimes a bit more of the face as the figure swayed slightly to and fro. It was an adult, and Harry was almost certain it was his man. He felt his excitement rise as the end of the hunt loomed into sight. But the target was not certain enough for a positive fatal shot, and a second or two later disappeared back into the house. Harry lowered the rifle but kept it close to hand in readiness.

It was half an hour before Rubeliev very suddenly emerged from the same doors, this time wearing a pair of loose swimming shorts. He took a couple of steps forward and, as Harry got his first clear aim, he suddenly turned and bent down as one of his young boys belted out of the doors and jumped into his father's now outstretched arms. "Shit!" muttered Harry under his breath, and he lowered the rifle a fraction so that he could better take in the whole scene.

Rubeliev was cuddling the boy and then began to swing him round and round by his arms. As the other boy ran out and demanded some attention, he grabbed hold of each by the hand and together they ran to the pool and jumped in. They emerged one after the other spluttering and gasping for breath, and Harry knew that sooner or later they would separate and he would get a clear shot.

After a minute or two of horsing around, Rubeliev began to move away from the boys to do some more serious swimming. At the far end of the pool, he stopped and leaned with his back against the side and his elbows outstretched behind him supported by the paved edge. He presented a perfect target. Harry raised the rifle once more and steadied his aim with the cross hairs of the sight centred on Rubeliev's head. He breathed out, emptying his lungs, and held his breath. At such a moment, time seems to pause and a quiet stillness descends. He put on first pressure, squeezing gently on the trigger.

At that very moment, the silence was broken as Harry heard a loud cough from somewhere close by. Instinctively, he took a sharp intake of breath and took his eye slightly away from the sight, cocking his ear to one side. There it was again, another cough and some talking. People were most definitely moving around downstairs.

His first instinct was to finish the job. He might never get a better chance. But when he took sight again, Rubeliev had pushed off from the end of the pool and was swimming back towards the boys. Harry took aim once more as the head and body alternately bobbed in and out of the water.

But the sounds from downstairs increased and he suddenly realised that, even with the noise suppressor, a shot would be heard, followed no doubt by screams from the children and others in the house. And his exit would be barred.

Harry cursed again but decided that whoever the men were, they were unlikely to stay around very long and he should get another opportunity when they had gone. He blamed himself that he had not practised disassembling the rifle, but it was extremely simple and he had it away in its briefcase within seconds. Case in hand, he dived under one of the trestles amid piles of plasterboard and pulled over a large empty box to give him some extra cover. He lay, with his pulse rate increasing, as the Russian chatter grew louder and he heard the sound of footsteps slowly mounting the stairs. He closed his hand around the butt of the pistol in its holster and waited.

The talking ceased as the two men went separate ways. One of them coughed again as he approached. He stopped at the window opening very close to Harry, presumably watching the family in the swimming pool, muttering something Harry could not understand. He heard a match being struck and soon the smell of tobacco told him that the man had lit up a cigarette.

Suddenly he heard a metallic sound and saw a large bunch of keys clatter onto the concrete floor just a couple of feet away from him. He took the gun from the holster and slowly thumbed across the safety catch. The man cursed in Russian and his nose appeared below the plasterboard, then the full profile of his face. Harry tensed, but the man was concentrating on the keys, which he fumbled, and then retrieved without looking to the side.

He remained at the window, muttering and coughing, until he had finished his cigarette and stubbed it out on the dusty concrete. His partner joined him and the two of them moved away to finish their tour of the first floor. By now, Harry had guessed that these were security guards, charged with making inspection rounds every so often throughout the weekend. He would lie low until they had left, and await a second chance.

Then, suddenly, his heart leapt. Harry wondered what the guards had made of the unlocked padlock. The way they were acting suggested that they had accepted it simply as slack security on the part of the builders. They may well report it, but Harry would be long gone by then.

But then a more serious problem hit him. They would most certainly lock the doors as they left. Even if he did get another opportunity to make a successful kill, he would have no way of making a quick getaway. He still had the key in his pocket but he would have no way of opening the padlock from the inside. He would be completely trapped within the site.

And this led to a further, even more pressing thought. If he were to get away at all, he would have to do so before the guards secured the site. They had now started up to the second floor, and this might be his only opportunity. "Shit, Shit, Shit" exclaimed Harry under his breath. He was not given to much swearing, but he did so now for the third time that morning.

He quickly wriggled his way out from under the trestle, a number of scenarios coursing through his mind. He had been so close to success. Would he get such a good opportunity again? He took a quick look out of the window but could only see a woman in the pool with the boys. There was no sign of Rubeliev. He might reappear of course and, if he could take out the watchmen, he might still get a second chance.

But he was no Jack Reacher. He had no mandate for further kills and he had no stomach to take innocent lives. In any case, there were two of them, doubtless with guns of their own, and there was no certainty of success. He decided that he had no option but to attempt to withdraw safely, with his identity intact, to await another opportunity.

He moved as quietly as possible down the stairs, out of the front door and across the site. It was only as he reached the entrance gate that he heard a loud shout of "Stoy" as he was spotted from a second-floor window.

There was no way that either of them was going to catch Harry now. He crossed the road, slung the briefcase in the rear seat and drove off. He was a good couple of hundred yards down the road before he caught sight of one of them in the rear mirror standing in the middle of the road, with a gun in one hand and the other on his hip, watching him speeding into the distance. A hundred yards or so behind him, Rubeliev's gatemen had also come out into the road to see what was happening.

Harry slowed down as he joined the busier traffic on the main highway and arrived back at the hotel ten minutes later without incident, breathing a long sigh of relief.

Making sure there was nobody around, Harry hid the briefcase away in the boot and went up to the room. Disappointed that Tatyana was not there, he took off his clothes and entered the shower to rid himself of the sweat of excitement and the grime of his sleep amongst the building materials. He let the soothing water play over his body as he gloomily mulled over the missed opportunity, helped only by the thought that the sound of a cough had allowed him to escape unharmed and with his cover still intact.

Chapter 12

Tatyana returned as Harry was dressing. She had not been able to sleep again but had gone downstairs to force down a light breakfast. She could see immediately from his face that things had not gone to plan and threw her arms around him. His shirt was still only half on and his arms were pinned down to his side. They remained locked together like that for a few moments before she asked, "What happened, Harry?"

"It's OK, darling," he immediately reassured her. "I'm not hurt and I managed to get away, but I didn't get him." After a short pause, he added ruefully, "I had him in my sights, Tania. It was so very close."

The remainder of the day was a sombre affair, each of them lost in their own different thoughts. With one near disaster, Tatyana wanted to abort the job right now, but Harry was so disappointed she felt that could not voice it - not today at least.

The same thought had occurred to Harry, but his concern revolved more around the awkward telephone conversation he would need to have with Giovanni, and he soon managed to put all thoughts of failure out of his mind and concentrate on new lines of attack. He still had the key to the building site and a repeat effort next Sunday was a possibility, but he soon discarded this idea as too dangerous. The security of the site was certain to be beefed up, and probably the padlock changed. Rubeliev himself would undoubtedly have been informed of the break-in and would be sorting out additional security for himself and his family.

Options seemed to be running out rapidly, thought Harry. He may have to take impulsive and perhaps more dangerous chances if he was to succeed. He was beginning once more to wish Tatyana was safely back in England, but he didn't fancy his chances of changing her mind now.

That evening, to relieve their disappointment, they decided to visit an Indian restaurant in Barvikha that had been recommended by a woman Tatyana had met in the gym. As they emerged from the lift, they heard an argument going on in the reception hall. Harry immediately recognised Rubeliev himself, who seemed to be calm enough, being harangued by the Hotel Manager whose voice was raised and who was making wild gestures with both hands. He was not sure whether Tatyana had recognised Rubeliev but said nothing as they continued through the main doors. Outside, a large Mercedes was parked immediately in front of the hotel with its engine running. In the back, the head of a woman Harry recognised as Rubeliev's wife turned to look at them briefly, and then looked away. A forty-odd-year-old brunette with a sweet oval face, she was much more attractive than the poor photos he had been given. She was waiting for her husband.

Without breaking step, they continued walking to their car. Harry whispered to Tatyana, "Sorry, darling. Dinner's off." Once in the car, he explained his remark. The Rubelievs appeared to be going out and, at this time of the evening, it would undoubtedly be for the theatre or perhaps dinner. An opportunity for him might arise, a toilet visit perhaps, and he had decided to follow them. His hand moved inside his jacket as he checked that the pistol was secure in its holster. Harry started the car and moved it slowly to a new parking spot where they could follow any movement of the Rubeliev car. He could see a chauffeur and another man in the front and assumed that the Rubelievs would be sitting together in the back.

It was more than five minutes before a stern looking Rubeliev appeared and joined his wife in the car, which then moved off. Harry waited until they were out of sight before he started to follow, soon picking up the very distinctive car. They were travelling east along the Rublevo-Uspenskoe Highway towards Moscow city centre.

Harry had become reasonably skilful over the years at shadowing his prey, both on foot and in a car, and found no difficulty in keeping up to four cars between him and the Mercedes in the steady traffic of the Highway. He took closer order, however, as the large junction at the end of the Highway approached. As he had expected, the Mercedes turned towards the city centre and the traffic became more congested.

Soon, they were driving along a wide avenue with four-lane carriageways separated by wide areas of grass and trees. Harry could see the Triumphal Arch in the distance when he was suddenly caught out by traffic lights turning red. He leaned forward, urging the car in front to go through, but it slowed and stopped leaving him no option but to stop himself. It was an agonizing wait but, being the main thoroughfare, it did not last too long. Harry managed to manoeuvre past the car in front and drove rather faster than he would have liked. A couple of minutes later they caught up with the main stream of traffic, and it was Tatyana who spotted the Merc about five cars in front, now on the inside lane with its right turn indicator winking. Harry slowed down and moved into the same lane.

Allowing some distance between them, Harry followed around the corner and could see the Merc parked about a hundred yards further along. As he drove by, the Rubelievs emerged from the car and headed towards a restaurant. Harry drove on another fifty yards or so, turned into a side road and managed to find a parking spot. They waited there briefly, half expecting the chauffeur to drive to the same area. When no car appeared, they got out and walked round the corner to see that the Merc had already disappeared from the front of the restaurant.

Massive stone office buildings dominate the area, with shops, showrooms and eating places of all sorts on the ground floor. The French restaurant that the Rubelievs had entered looked particularly elegant with its green Dutch awnings over each window, tastefully emblazoned with the word "Maxims". Underneath each window was a wrought iron trough full of colourful flowers.

As they entered, Harry smiled at Tatyana and whispered, "Dinner's back on again, darling. An expensive one by the looks of it." The restaurant was quite full, and he wondered whether they would be able to get a table without a reservation. It might require a sweetener, he thought, and took out a couple of notes from his wallet. They had to wait by the door for some time because the Rubelievs' table was surrounded by an army of waiters fluffing out napkins and handing out menus, all orchestrated by the Maître D. Clearly, they were frequent and most favoured clients.

As they waited, Harry spotted a table for two that would command a good view of the Rubeliev table but was close to the door should they need to make a speedy exit. As he edged towards the table, he was spotted by the Maître D who excused himself to Rubeliev and came towards them with a welcoming smile. Harry made a gesture towards the table as if to say "Is this table free?" The Maître consulted a list earnestly, pursing his lips and shaking his head slowly but, the moment he felt Harry's banknotes in his hand, he nodded, smiled once more and pulled out a chair inviting Tatyana to be seated. Almost immediately a wine waiter appeared to ask whether they would like a drink before their meal. Harry ordered a Ricard and a Kir for Tatyana, and they settled to await events.

They did not have to wait long. Within a couple of minutes, and without any warning, it was a most unwelcome event. The entrance door opened and in strode Pock-man, the man who had passed them on their very first day as they had been studying the building site notices. But this time, perhaps because of a connection with Rubeliev who was sitting just a few feet away, Harry placed the man instantly. He realised that he had never actually met or seen him at all, but had recognised the face from blurred photographs in Fossen's dossier. And he was one of Rubeliev's security men.

Pock-man walked swiftly past their table, but then he stopped abruptly and his head snapped round sharply to look at them. Harry bent and whispered to Tatyana as nonchalantly as he could muster, "I think dinner may be off again, darling." Tatyana looked a bit puzzled. She had been studying the menu and had not made the connection.

The man paused for only a couple of seconds, then headed purposely for Rubeliev's table where he bent down and whispered into Rubeliev's ear at some length. They both looked up and stared in their direction. With his eyes firmly fixed on Harry, Rubeliev issued some orders to the man, who then disappeared through a service door.

This was enough for Harry. They had to get out now – and quickly. The thought flashed through his mind that perhaps he should take out Rubeliev first. But the place was too crowded to be sure of a kill from where he was, so he would have to get much closer. Rubeliev was probably armed, as certainly would be his bodyguard, who would reappear at any moment. He decided immediately that it would be too dangerous - both for him, more especially for Tatyana.

Harry leaned over and spoke to her urgently, "We have to leave right now. If a waiter asks, tell him I am not feeling well and need some air. Come on. Quick!"

Rubeliev was rising from his chair as they got up and walked hurriedly to the door. Outside, it was beginning to get dark and Harry instinctively turned right towards the main highway, which was better lit . There was nobody about and it was eerie in these side streets. It should be easier to lose a pursuer in a busier, more public environment. But this was Sunday evening in a mainly business area and, even as they approached the highway, there were not many people about. He looked back and saw Rubeliev and his security guard outside the restaurant gesticulating to a couple of waiters who were throwing aside their aprons as they all started to run after them.

Harry and Tatyana had been walking quickly up to this point, but now Tatyana kicked off her high heels and they started to run. They were cut off from retrieving their car now, but both were familiar with the area and Harry knew that the Park Pobedy Metro Station was nearby. He soon spotted one of the entrances and shouted to Tatyana that this seemed to be their best bet. They would not have time to buy a ticket, so they would have to leap over the automatic machines. This would have the advantage of alerting the Metro police, which should muddy the waters if they began to give chase too. And, if all else failed, he would rather give himself up to the police than to Rubeliev and his men.

The entrance led down into a grand hall, where the two of them raced for the ticketed entrance machines and vaulted over them to the surprise of the few passengers around. The elderly ticket collector shouted at them to stop, and then immediately lifted a telephone on the wall behind him. By this time, they were both on the escalator and Harry groaned out loud. Of all the escalators in the entire world, he just had to have picked the longest and deepest. So long is it, at well over a hundred metres, that he could not see to the bottom of the arched tunnel, lit by hundreds of brilliant globes of light.

They raced down as fast as they could, nudging their way past the occasional passenger. About three-quarters of the way down, Harry heard a train pulling into one of the platforms, but by the time they had reached the bottom it had taken on its passengers and they were only in time to see the doors closing and the train starting to move away. They found themselves in a long hall between the platforms, clad in brown and white marble with a glistening grey and white granite floor. At either end were brightly coloured enamel panels celebrating two wars.

They noticed little of this, however. Harry turned to wait for Tatyana who had fallen a little behind and saw Pock-man well in the lead of the chasing group more than half way down the escalator. He took hold of Tatyana's hand and led her onto the other platform, colliding into and almost knocking over an ancient railway employee who had been slowly sweeping the floor. As they raced along the platform, Harry spotted a couple of doors set into the marble walls just before the next exit. He rattled the first one, but it was locked. He spotted the key sticking from the lock of the second. He swiftly opened the door, removed the key, bundled himself and Tatyana inside, and locked the door from the inside.

It was pitch black, and they clung to each other trying to catch their breath as quietly as possible. After fifteen seconds or so they heard footsteps running down the platform. The first door was rattled, then the door they were behind. Feet scuffled and men started talking, but Tatyana could not hear the words well enough to understand what they were saying. After a while, they heard the sounds of feet moving away.

They stayed clinging together until they had both regained most of their breath and some of their composure. Harry felt for a light switch but gave up when he had second thoughts. It might be visible from outside. He remembered that he had a small LED torch on his key ring, which he fished out of his pocket. He played the torch on Tatyana's face. It showed signs of sweat from her exertions but she seemed calm enough, and his heart leapt out to her as she smiled gently at him.

He started to shine the torch slowly round the small room. Shelves which lined the far wall were stacked with cleaning materials of all kinds. A tall cabinet with a small key left in the lock, seemingly a Russian habit. Next to that was…

"Oh, my God!" Harry exclaimed in shock, but almost in a whisper. Tatyana started to scream but managed to stifle it by covering her mouth. A corpse, its toothless mouth and sunken eyes wide open stared up at them. Harry turned off the torch and said quietly, "Look away, darling."

He switched the torch back on to examine the body. Suddenly, he saw its eyes blink and then heard a frail noise coming from the mouth. It was a very old man, slouched in an equally old armchair. Harry placed one hand over the man's mouth and put one finger of his other hand to his lips. "Shhhh," he mouthed. The man ceased trying to cry out for help but began to sob quietly.

He was only half dressed in what might have been a railway uniform of some kind. Harry guessed that he had been sleeping when they barged in and woke him. To his right were the vestiges of a snack and a dirty cup. He may have just been on a break, but this might be where he lived, thought Harry.

Recovering her composure, Tatyana bent over to reassure him. They meant him no harm, she told him, and they would be gone before long. The three of them stayed like that for several minutes as they listened to the different patterns of footsteps on the platform outside, and a couple of trains arrive and depart. Harry whispered to Tatyana, "The next train that comes in. We'll wait until it has completely stopped, then make a dash for it. OK?"

"OK," she agreed.

It was several minutes more before they heard the rumble of another train arriving. Harry took hold of the key in one hand. As the train slowed to a stop, he whispered, "Ready," and a moment later turned the key and burst open the door.

The very moment it was open, all hope of escape disappeared in a flash. Other hands took charge of the door. Harry felt himself being dragged out onto the platform, scuffling and punching to escape their hold, and then a sharp pin prick in his hand. He tried to look around for Tatyana but instead succumbed slowly, inexorably, into a deep, deep blackness...

Chapter 13

Tatyana's eyelids flickered briefly. She had a bitter taste in her mouth, but she found that she could not move her tongue to bathe it. Nor could she move her head. She could shift her body very slightly, but not her legs or her arms. She was trapped in her body. Was she paralysed? Or was she perhaps already dead?

Slowly, mistily at first, her eyes began to open fully. She was in a small room she had never seen before. But all she could focus on was just a few feet immediately in front of her. In a sturdy chair was the slumped body of the man she loved. All his limbs were firmly secured to the chair with industrial black duct tape, as was the chest upon which his chin was now resting. All Tatyana could see of his head was the mop of curly dark brown hair she had run her hands through so often. She had no idea how long it would be before he came round, and felt herself moving once more into semi-consciousness.

She was very frightened. Again, she tried to move her arms and legs, but they were firmly secured. She soon began to realise that her rising anxiety was putting too much strain on her restricted breathing. She had to calm herself if she was to stay awake for Harry.

It was more than a quarter of an hour before he showed any signs of life. He raised his head, shaking it violently, attempting to emerge from the drug-induced stupor, clearing spittle from his lips and trying to rid his mouth of a bitter taste.

His eyelids felt so very heavy. After several attempts, he managed to keep them open and very gradually begin to focus. He croaked out loud, "Tania. Darling," as he caught sight of her. She was seated in something that reminded him of an ancient dentist's chair. All her limbs were secured by clamps to the arms and legs of the chilling contraption. Her head was similarly held by other clamps that were attached to a bar that appeared to come from within the ceiling. Her mouth was being held open by a red ball fastened by straps around her neck. Her blond tresses were matted with sweat and hung limply around her shoulders. Her eyes stared wildly at him but strangely, Harry felt, more in sadness than in terror. His heart groaned.

"Tania" he cried out again and, as he did so, two men entered the room. Viktor Rubeliev sat down in a chair behind a desk to Harry's right. The other man he recognised from a photograph was Rubeliev's right-hand man, Vladimir Mussorgsky.

Neither man spoke for a while, but they both studied their captives intently. Finally, Rubeliev started with unexpected formality, "Good morning, Mr Fletcher."

After a short pause, he continued quietly and simply, "Why do you wish to kill me?"

"I haven't a clue what you're talking about." Harry croaked.

Rubeliev sighed. "I understand your confusion. You have only just woken up." He paused, either to give Harry time to recover or to gather his thoughts.

Finally, he continued, "Once your head is clear, I think you will realise that neither of you is likely to leave this room alive. Whether you, or more particularly your friend here, suffer terrible pain before you die is entirely up to you. Before I ask you again, let me give you some information and some advice. Yegor, my senior security man has seen you twice, once at my home and once at the restaurant last night. Co-incidence?... Possibly."

He rose to sit on the edge of the desk and slapped down a series of photographs one by one. "You see these? We have security pictures of you both entering and running away from the building site next to my house. And I have seen the report the security watchmen gave to the police".

Leaving the pictures scattered on the desk, he stood up and went to sit behind it once again. "There were times last night when my driver was concerned that we were being followed. I remember him mentioning it at the time. And then, early this morning, we found a car hired under your name parked around the corner from the restaurant. In the boot, we found... a rifle."

He paused, then continued, "Oh, and of course we discovered this little beast on you." He took the PSS pistol from a drawer and placed it on the desk, looked up at Harry and said, "Not the sort of thing an ordinary Englishman would normally walk around with I think you'll agree."

"So you see, Fletcher, denial is completely futile. I cannot think why you should hold a personal grudge against me, so I have to assume that you are professional, and all that we need from you is – who hired you, and why..."

Harry did not reply immediately. Rubeliev said, "That's right. Give it some thought. We have plenty of time"

It was a hundred thoughts that raced through Harry's mind. He had been clumsy, and it was clear that they had far too much evidence for him to continue denial. His own life, he knew, was as good as over. But perhaps could save Tatyana.

"OK," he sighed. "I concede. It's true. I do have a contract." He paused briefly to catch his breath and gather his thoughts and then continued, "But this girl knew nothing about it. She is just a companion - I was using her as cover. It would be most unfair if you were to hurt her in any way."

"I said that we have plenty of time, Fletcher, but I will not have it wasted. Whatever 'this girl', as you call her, is - she is more than just an innocent bit of cover. She is your accomplice, and she will bear the consequences. Now, answer my question, man. Who hired you, and why?"

As Rubeliev was saying this, Mussorgsky got up and moved to the chair that held Tatyana prisoner. Roughly, he unbuttoned the white blouse she had put on for the dinner that never was the previous evening, and flicked it wide open. One side slipped back over her body but the other remained open leaving her right breast exposed.

Harry groaned, surprised that there was no bra. Surely she would not have gone out without one. Rubeliev must have read his thoughts. "You were both strip searched whilst you were asleep," he explained. "They only put back on the essentials."

Harry remained silent as Mussorgsky opened a cupboard and took out a leather wrap which he spread out on the desk. Tatyana could not move her head from side to side, but her eyes moved to the sides of their sockets in terror. She could just make out the array of horrific-looking instruments that resembled a mixture of DIY and medical equipment. Harry groaned out loud once again.

"Harry Fletcher," Rubeliev began again, "you and I have much in common you know. We have both chosen unusual careers. We both perform acts that would repulse most people, and we do it because it pays us well. We live by the sword, but we should also be prepared to die by the sword. And now, my friend, it is your turn, and that of your girl." After a short pause, he continued in a more earnest tone, "Cut the crap, Harry. I assure you neither of us enjoys inflicting pain. But you must understand that I simply have to know who my enemies are."

Again, he paused for effect and then bent down towards Harry and continued gravely, "Given that you both have very few minutes left on this Earth, your girl will have no more use for her nipple. It is surely therefore only the manner of her losing it that should concern you."

As he said this, Mussorgsky selected what looked like an oversize pair of pliers and a scalpel and moved towards Tatyana, who looked to be close to fainting.

Harry shouted out, "No. No." And he then added, more quietly. "No. I'll tell you."

The words tumbled out of Harry's mouth, "It was an American, Giovanni Pollini."

Rubeliev was visibly shaken. His body shot upright and he leant back. "Giovanni?" he questioned. "Giovanni Pollini?" he repeated, and then turned to Mussorgsky. "I thought I knew him well, Vova."

He paused for a moment and then continued more quietly, "I was surprised he even wanted the job. But this..." He shook his head and went deep into thought.

After a while, he turned to Harry and asked, "Did you meet with Giovanni in person when he offered you this contract?"

"Yes. In Naples, Italy," said Harry.

"How was he? How did he seem? Was he alone?"

Harry paused, collecting his thoughts. "He seemed fair enough. He was emotional, of course, when he told me about his brother's cancer. I assume you know all about that."

Rubeliev remained silent. Harry's head was swimming. He hadn't fully recovered yet but he continued haltingly, "I've known him a long time you know. I'm not sure what you want from me. I must say, he didn't seem to relish very much the idea of taking over from his brother. Perhaps he just feels he must try to keep the job in the family," then he added, "or at least for an American.

Rubeliev asked again, "Did he have anyone with him?"

"Yes. He had his... lawyer, I think he said he was. I remember he also talked about him as his minder."

Rubeliev leaned forward, "Do you remember his name?"

"Er yes... Fossen. Carl Fossen."

A broad smile spread slowly over Rubeliev's face, and it echoed on Mussorgsky's face as they looked at each other knowingly. Rubeliev sat back in his chair with a satisfied grin, which then gradually faded as he entered another period of thought.

It was some time before he seemed to recover and returned once more to Harry and Tatyana. He looked intently at each of them, slowly from one to the other.

"Ah well," he sighed. "That's it then." His hand moved to one of the buttons on his desk, and Harry screamed as the infernal killing machine whirred into life.

Chapter 14

In Las Vegas, Carl Fossen's ears should have been burning. As Harry had revealed his name, it had rung several bells in the minds of both Rubeliev and Mussorgsky. They did have quite a file on him, but certainly not the whole story.

Carl Fossen's grandparents had emigrated from Germany soon after the Second World War. His father had served in the Wehrmacht and had been fortunate enough to survive Operation Barbarossa, escaping from the Russians and making his way back to Germany. His wife had been a much more enthusiastic supporter of Hitler and had joined the League of German Girls where she was later recruited as a Concentration Camp guard, eventually serving in Ravensbrück and other camps. After the liberation, she was detained at the Recklinghausen Internment Camp but never put on trial and was released after only a few months.

They had decided to start life afresh and emigrated to America. They finally settled in California, on the outskirts of Los Angeles, where they opened a small shop selling and repairing all types of clocks and watches. Living in an apartment over the shop, she eventually gave birth to a son, Paul. They were conscientious and felt they could only afford to have one child, and they had seriously spoiled him. Despite their poverty, they gave him anything he desired, and he repaid them by failing to work at High School and flunking his College exams. He drifted around, still largely funded by his parents, and eventually turned to gambling to feed a growing drug habit.

After a furious row with his parents, he left home and set up in Las Vegas, the Mecca for all gamblers and many drug addicts. There, he did manage to buckle down to a few rather menial jobs, but only to fuel the gambling and drugs. He also met and married a croupier, a headstrong girl who took full advantage of the weak young man and bullied him mercilessly. It was not a happy marriage but did produce a son, Carl.

The poor boy stood little chance from the outset. He was bullied throughout his early school days and went home to a father he despised because he was so penniless and weak, and to a mother who always had a drink in her hand and terrorised both of them. It may have been the latter that founded his lifelong dislike of women and established his sexual orientation.

He was determined not to make the same mistakes as his father. He worked hard at all levels of school, easing his way through to Senior High School from where he graduated with straight As.

Along with all this academic work, he was careful not to neglect the care and development of his body, working out hard in the gym and signing up for the football and boxing teams. He was not a tall boy and did not prove to possess any great natural sporting ability, but made up for this with the same sort of dogged aggressiveness that he applied to his academic work. He drank little and steered well clear of all drugs. This approach, along with a rather dour personality, failed to attract many friendships, and he became something of a loner throughout his Senior High School years.

Upon graduation, he went on to win a scholarship to study Criminal Law at the University of Las Vegas. By this time, his parents had long been separated, and he had ceased to have any contact with either of them. Whilst the scholarship covered all the tuition fees, there was little left to live on, and Carl realised that he would have to find a way to finance his rent and daily living expenses.

In a typically pragmatic fashion, he decided to make use of his gay sexuality and managed to track down a private agency for high-class male prostitution. The work came easy to him and paid well. His looks were passable and his body was fit and muscular, so he soon established a core list of regular clients. Whilst his peers at university were sweating away for long hours in restaurants and bars, this provided him with rent for a good apartment and generous spending money.

A particular episode arose after about six months. The agency offered him a party at one of the large hotels on The Strip. This was not an uncommon sort of gig that involved sex of some description with any man who was attracted to him. Carl was always rather wary of such assignments since they frequently involved sexual violence, and on more than one occasion he had had to call on his physical strength and boxing experience to extricate himself. However, they did pay very well and he agreed to take the job.

On arrival, the hotel reception arranged for a bellboy to accompany him to one of the largest suites Carl had ever seen. Once inside, he spotted a fellow professional who he knew well, along with two men that he did not recognise. It took him only a few seconds to realise that this was the full complement for the party.

One of the men came forward introducing himself as Stavros. If his name failed to disclose his origins, then his heavy accent and looks certainly did. Although he had the swarthy appearance of a southern European, he was no Greek God. His heavily pockmarked face was inhabited by overlarge features and, as he now advanced towards Carl, his smile revealed an array of gold teeth. As he smiled a greeting, Carl inwardly groaned - but it went with the job.

He shook Carl's hand warmly and led him over to his companion. "Let me introduce you to Rico," he said. Then, as they shook hands, he added, "and I believe you know Michael." Carl nodded to his friend.

In complete contrast to Stavros, his friend enjoyed the looks of some Hollywood heartthrob. Indeed, Carl wondered for a moment whether he had perhaps jetted in from Los Angeles, as he experienced some vague suspicion that he recognised him. A generous wide mouth dominated his tanned face, and a lock of stray black hair flopped over his left eye. Deep brown eyes twinkled in the room's bright lights, promising a vivacious and generous personality.

The afternoon followed a well-trodden path. Stavros served drinks which Carl guessed defined him as the host. This would mean that Rico would get the first pick, and Carl decided very early that he would use his best flirtatious powers to make sure it was he that he picked.

Sometimes, sport or pornographic movies were played on the television, but on this occasion they chatted for a while and, after a couple of drinks, Rico called Carl over to sit beside him on his sofa. His decision had been made and, after one more drink, Rico announced that it was time for them to become better acquainted and led Carl to one of the two bedrooms.

Carl was relieved that the required sex turned out to be of the straight oral and anal varieties, and Rico turned out to be a gentle and attentive lover. They were both very satisfied and it was nearly two hours before they emerged from the bedroom, only to find Stavros alone watching television. He did not explain why Michael had left.

When he came to leave, Rico kissed him and asked Carl if he could see him again. Carl said that he was happy to do so but that, for contractual reasons, it would have to be arranged through the agency. Rico seemed somewhat annoyed by this but said he would take care of things.

The next evening, his agent telephoned giving him another date with Rico and then, with an apology, made the surprise announcement that he had removed Carl from the agency's list of escorts. This alarmed Carl, who saw it as a serious threat to his income, and he took it up with Rico when they met.

"I'm sorry Carl," Rico said. "I should have talked it over with you first. The thing is, we seemed to get on real great the other day and I felt we could have something special between us. I don't know if you agree." Carl took this as a statement rather than a question and remained silent.

"Now, I have to go away quite a bit," Rico continued, "and I'd like you to be around whenever I am here. I'd like us to get real pally. And I don't want you screwing around while I'm gone. See?"

Carl still didn't reply, so he continued, "Money's no problem, Carl. Money I have. I'll rent a swell place where we can be together, and I'll give you a good allowance so that you can get on with your study without any worries – I want you to do that. I think it's great."

He paused for a moment and then asked, "Whatcha say?"

Carl didn't have to think for very long. He liked the man and they had good sex. It also represented a step up in life and would secure hassle-free financial security. What did he have to lose?

"OK, Rico. Let's give it a go."

"Awesome," said Rico, and with that, the shape of Carl's life was decided for the next several years. Rico was indeed frequently away, sometimes for lengthy periods, and Carl found himself missing him when he was gone. But Rico did write to him regularly and telephoned if he was away for more than a couple of nights.

Carl also missed any public demonstration of their relationship. Rico had rented a small but luxurious penthouse within a fully secure environment, just off The Strip. Carl could come and go as he pleased, but Rico always arrived by car straight into the basement parking lot, and then up by the internal elevator. They never left together, and only very rarely did they arrange to meet away from the building. Their liaison remained almost entirely private. But they did enjoy a good relaxed life together, and Carl never queried this odd arrangement.

The relationship continued for the whole period of Carl's university studies, but soon after graduation, it was curtailed just as suddenly as it had begun.

Rico had been somewhat subdued for several months, and visited Carl increasingly irregularly, with telephone calls and letters drying up almost completely. It came as no great surprise to Carl, therefore, when one evening after they had made love Rico announced that it had been for the last time. Naturally, Carl had been upset and had asked why. What had happened? Was it him? All the usual questions.

"Nah. Nah," Rico assured him. "It's just... well... I'm starting a new chunk of my life, Carl, and you and me – we just don't seem to fit into it somehow. I'm real sorry. We've had a great time and I'm still very fond of you. Remember that."

Carl was saddened but could think of nothing to say. He knew instinctively that there was no point in any protest. After a few moments' silence, Rico continued, "You've got your degree now, and you're a bright kid. I know you'll do just fine. And I've arranged a start for you – how about Junior Exec in one of the largest organisations running casinos in Las Vegas? Go see this guy next Tuesday - 10am. OK?"

He handed Carl a sheet of paper, printed on both sides, with information about the company and the name of the man he was to see at the top. Carl took it, looked briefly at it, folded it, and said quietly, "Thanks, Rico."

"Come on. Cheer up, man. The rest of your life is just starting," Rico encouraged him. "Oh, and I've arranged for the rent of this place to be paid for twelve months. Right?"

With that, Rico went over to Carl and kissed him chastely, placed his apartment key down on the sideboard, and left with a hand in the air and a simple, "Bye Carl. Good luck."

From the very moment that door closed, Carl devoted himself to a tireless search for power and wealth. It was in his first week at the Vegas Casinos Corp that he learned of Rico's real identity. Ricardo was the youngest son of the Capo, Don, Godfather or whatever you choose to call the Boss of Bosses in the worldwide Mafia organisation. He found that he was neither shocked nor even particularly surprised. It explained the secret nature of their relationship and fitted well with the personality of the man he had known so intimately.

What did surprise him shortly afterwards, however, was the announcement in the gossip column of the Las Vegas Review-Journal that Riccardo Pollini and his new wife, Jackie Perkins, described somewhat flatteringly as a Hollywood film actress, were expecting the birth of their first child early in the New Year. This threw Carl at first. He simply did not know how to take the news. He felt cheated. Were the last few years just one big lie?

It was sometime later that he came to understand. Whilst Rico may well be bi-sexual, the reason behind this new form of relationship was political – at least in part. For a man in his position, it was more acceptable to have a wife and children, an all-American heterosexual family man.

This prompted a further thought, which in turn led to a hallmark action which was to become fundamental to his rise to the very top echelons of the Organisation. He began compiling a dossier from letters, photographs and other pieces of memorabilia relating to their liaison. The most telling item was a rather graphic video they had made of their love-making early on in their relationship, which he thought Rico may well have forgotten. When complete, the dossier was lodged in a local secure vault, along with detailed instructions regarding how it should be released in the case of his death. This then became a template for more than a dozen similar dossiers, many of which would come to be used over the coming years to enforce his will.

To Carl's surprise, Rico eventually succeeded his father rather than his elder brother. Deciding he would be better placed if he were closer to Rico, he tried to arrange a meeting between the two of them. Instead of a direct reply, Rico sent one of his aides to see Carl with a very polite, but equally firm, message that the past should remain in the past. Rico well appreciated Carl's work, but he would not be meeting with him.

This rebuff steeled Carl's resolve and further drove his relentless march to the very top, not only of his Casino Corp but of many other Mafia-controlled activities in the Las Vegas area.

He remained a loner. His contacts list was as long as anyone in the state of Nevada, but it included no real friends. His private black book included telephone numbers of a variety of sexual partners. His sexual preferences had turned ever more violent which resulted in few long-term relationships. Most of the names were, therefore, professionals, rather than friends.

When he learned of Rico's illness, his first thought was of the opportunity it might provide, rather than any great sorrow for his one-time lover. However, he did possess sufficient self-awareness to realise that he would never succeed to the very highest post. He was respected, but it was founded on fear, not the love that makes a Boss of Bosses.

Thus, his mind turned to the idea of acting as a king-maker, and he soon decided that the role of the power behind the throne would suit him perfectly. He was not surprised when Roy Becker, to whom he had never related, made the first move in almost indecent taste. Later, when the Russian's name was put forward, his target was suddenly thrown into a clear, brilliant spotlight.

He had met Giovanni on innumerable occasions, of course, but they could hardly be called close. He arranged a meeting, only to find that Giovanni had never even considered entering the fray. Moreover, when Carl put it to him that there was no other suitable American candidate, and that a Russian might well be elected, he had merely shrugged and said, "That's progress I guess, Carl." This had not discouraged Carl who piled on the pressure, insisting that it was his duty to prolong the family's reign.

"No. No, Carl. I'm too old. The job needs a younger man. And I don't believe I have sufficient support. So - thank you, but no thank you, Carl"

"But it's your family, Giovanni. Isn't that important to you?"

"Sure. 'Cause it is. But, as I said, I'm too old, and there ain't no one else in the family now."

"Well, I'm pretty well family. And I care a lot..."

"What the do you mean 'you're pretty well family'? You're talking about the Mafia family - huh?"

"No. Much more than that, Giovanni. I'm taking about the Pollini family. I lived with your brother, Rico, for almost three years. We were lovers. We had a good close relati..."

"What the fuck are you talking about?" Giovanni interrupted. "You saying my brother's gay? He is not and never has been. He's married with kids, for Chris' sake."

"I'm sorry, Giovanni. But it's all true. And I have proof." He fumbled in his briefcase and drew out a fat file in a thick bright red cover.

"I don't believe one word of it." Giovanni exploded with anger, his face now as red as the folder. "You're a fucking liar."

"It's all there," Carl insisted as he dropped the dossier onto the coffee table. "That's a copy. The original's in a bank vault," and after a short pause he added, "with instructions to publish if anything happens to me."

"Get the fuck out, you lying little prick," Giovanni shouted, now quite beside himself.

Carl cowered and held up a hand. "OK. OK. I'm going...", as he turned to make a hurried, clumsy exit.

Giovanni stood still for a while, trying to regain his composure. Then he picked up the dossier, opened a drawer, threw it in and slammed the drawer shut.

It was less than a week later that he made arrangements for the two of them to meet with Harry Fletcher in Naples.

Chapter 15

In Rubeliev's killing room, the deadly apparatus continued to whirr. As it did so, it rose and entered the ceiling, the flap closing on it with a quiet metallic *blip*.

Her head now freed, Tatyana shook it to loosen her hair, but it was matted with sweat and stubbornly refused to frame her head as she liked. Any relief she felt did not show and she began to sob quietly. Rubeliev got up and went over to her. Without buttoning it, he flipped the loose blouse over to cover her nakedness. Then he reached round her neck, unbuckled the gag and removed the ball from her mouth. Finally, he dug into a drawer in his desk, took out a pack of tissues, and gently removed some of the sweat and grime from her face. He resumed the seat behind his desk with no mention of the apparent change of heart. There was no need - the threat remained as palpable as ever.

He whispered in Russian to Mussorgsky and then sat in silence thought for a while. Finally, he said, "I am going to leave you now. I need to do some thinking, and talk this over with my colleague here."

They both got to their feet and headed out of the room. As he reached the door, Rubeliev turned briefly and added, "As you've no doubt guessed, we'll be able to hear anything you say."

It was Tatyana who spoke first through her sobs, "I'm sorry, darling."

"Don't, my darling. It's not your fault. You'll be OK. Just try to keep calm."

"You could have got away if I hadn't been there."

"Stop it, darling - right now," said Harry sternly. "Just save your breath and calm down."

They didn't speak again. Instinctively, Harry tested the plastic ties that locked him to the chair, but unsurprisingly there was no play in them. There was nothing to do but try to relax and wait for whatever fate awaited them.

It seemed to them much longer, but they had only about a quarter of an hour to wait before Rubeliev returned alone. Instead of sitting behind the desk, he dragged Mussorgsky's chair to a position between Harry and Tatyana. He looked from one to the other and said, "You're not just partners in crime are you, my friends."

"If you must know, we're married," Harry started. "But I assure you she's nothing to do with my work, and knows nothing about the..."

Rubeliev nodded and held up a hand to interrupt him, "I'm not interested in your domestic arrangements. She was with you, and therefore complicit. That's enough for me."

Harry started to protest again, but Rubeliev put up his hand again to stop him.

"No. Keep quiet. Just listen. I have a proposition for you – an offer I believe you cannot refuse." He smiled and paused for a moment. "As I said earlier, we have a lot in common. We're professionals. But you, my friend, and me too probably, we've both been conned. I'm sure that Giovanni has no real interest in taking over control. It's that nasty little man, Carl Fossen. Somehow, he's managed to convince Giovanni that he should stand. It may be some form of blackmail. Maybe he's got some dirt on him. I don't know."

Again, he paused for thought. Then, "I want to buy the contract from Giovanni, just change the hit, from myself to Fossen. I'll pay you the same price." Then, after a short pause, he asked, "Incidentally, what was the price for my life?"

Harry didn't answer immediately, but couldn't think of a good reason not to tell him. "Three million pounds sterling," he said.

Rubeliev whistled and said, "I'm flattered."

Harry added, "Giovanni did send me half a million in advance..."

Rubeliev grinned and said, "You'll just have to reimburse him, won't you, Fletcher? You failed."

After a long pause, Rubeliev agreed, "OK. Two and a half million sounds exorbitant for that little shit's life, but I'll pay it. It won't be an easy job."

Then he continued, "But much more than that, of course, both of you will be walking away from here alive. My Deputy thinks I should keep your girl, I'm sorry – your wife, as a hostage. But I'm willing to trust you. I'm sure you know how long our arms can reach if you should decide to abuse my trust."

There was silence then. Harry's mind raced with the implications, but there seemed to be no contest. The man was offering them the chance to live. He had no illusions as to what fate would await them both if he refused the offer. And anyway, why should he? His own view of Fossen matched that of the Russian. It would not be difficult to justify the kill in his mind.

Harry's arms were still tethered to the chair, but he managed to lift a hand, offering it to Rubeliev who took it, smiled and said, "I thought you might." Tatyana relaxed visibly, her shoulders dropping as the tension began to dissolve and, with a little smile, she said quietly, "Thank you" to their captor.

"No need for thanks," Rubeliev said. "Your husband has taken on a most dangerous task - could be a death sentence in itself." He leaned behind himself and pressed a button to release the clamps holding Tatyana. She rose rubbing her arms and wrists to get the circulation going again, and fumbled with the buttons of her blouse. She then joined Rubeliev in ripping off the plastic bonds that secured Harry. When he was finally free, they hugged and kissed, but only briefly with Rubeliev looking on.

They followed him out of the room, through a bathroom into a large office cum living room. Mussorgsky was nowhere to be seen, so they assumed that he had already left. They were still massaging their limbs as Rubeliev waved them to sit on one of the sofas. He opened a cabinet, took out a bottle of Vodka, poured out three shots and carried them over, cupping the three glasses in one hand. He handed one to each of them, lifted his glass in their direction, and downed it in one. Tatyana coughed and spluttered as she followed suit. Harry gently slapped her on the back as he downed his.

Rubeliev perched on the arm of the other sofa and started to elaborate on his theory. He explained that he had spoken with Giovanni before putting his own name forward and, at that time at least, Giovanni certainly had no intention of entering the contest. He was, he had said, too old and tired to even consider it. Something, or somebody, had changed his mind, and Rubeliev was convinced that it was Fossen. And it was Fossen who would have been behind this senseless assassination attempt.

He claimed to have quite a large file on the man. He neither liked nor trusted him, and his investigations indicated that many of his stateside peers held similar views. There was even evidence of him blackmailing some of his fellow associates. He was a loner, totally ruthless, and dedicated to amassing power. If he did have anything on Giovanni, he would not hesitate to use it. And if Giovanni was elected, he would surely find himself in Fossen's pocket.

"If you've only met him one time, you won't know much about him. He's gay, and a very violent man. And that's often a dangerous combination." He hesitated for several moments and then continued.

"I'll tell you a story about Carl Fossen. It might help steel your resolve for your new target. I have no idea whether it's completely true. It could be an exaggeration, or it may be entirely made up, but at the very least it is one man's perception of what Fossen is capable of. It was recounted to a friend of my colleague you've just met by one of Fossen's gay partners - a Frenchman, Jules I think his name was. I'll repeat it to you exactly as I remember it."

"The two men had been together for more than a year and Fossen had been away from his Las Vegas apartment for some time. One day, he returned without notice and found Jules in bed with a casual lover - in his own apartment."

"I'm told that he's normally a character of little emotion, but Fossen immediately saw a violent shade of crimson. He ran past his partner and used his anger, his strength and some boxing training to lay the other man out cold. Jules meanwhile was cowering, muttering apologies and pleading for mercy. He remembers Fossen turning towards him, nursing his hand and shaking with rage."

"Oddly enough, he laid no hand on his lover. All his anger was channelled towards the other man - presumably convinced that he had taken advantage of his absence and seduced Jules. He seemed to calm down eventually, at least on the outside, but the rage grew and hardened within him. Vengeance must have festered in his mind and he went about planning his retribution coldly and calmly."

"They had loads of bondage gear, so he had no difficulty in securely immobilizing Jules' lover. The following morning, he left him in the care of Jules with the threat that if they were not both in the apartment when he returned, neither of them would live to see the day out. Jules knew that his partner was not prone to making idle threats, so had no choice but to stand guard over the man, who spent the time alternately crying and pleading to be allowed to go free."

"Fossen returned in the afternoon, took both of them down to his private basement car park and drove them out of town to an isolated collection of deserted buildings. Many years back it had been a gas station and diner, but the new highway had taken a very different route and it had been left to the mercies of the desert wind and sand."

"The diner wasn't in bad condition and was reasonably weather proof as Fossen unlocked the front door to let them in. As they entered, it was immediately apparent that Fossen had spent the day preparing the place for whatever charade was due to be played out that afternoon. It wasn't exactly clean. Dust and sand covered most of the surfaces and raised a small cloud from the floor with every footstep. But an attempt had certainly been made to tidy it up, and the main pieces of furniture were clean and even polished."

"The middle of the main floor had been cleared and was arranged for all the world like a theatrical stage set. In the centre was a table laid out for a meal for two. To the side of it was a trolley with a gas canister feeding a cooking ring, a chopping board, a couple of large plates, a set of knives and an array of barbeque cooking implements."

"It's time for your last supper, my friend," Fossen said calmly to the man he blamed for his lover's infidelity. Still shackled, he had been agitated enough during the journey, but the word "last" now raised his anxiety to new levels and he was shaking uncontrollably. As the man's distress increased, so Fossen became correspondingly serene. But it was a disquieting calmness, filled with the promise of impending violence."

"Jules too was showing more and more signs of distress, and these increased when he was instructed to strip the unfortunate man of all his clothes and to refasten the handcuffs behind his back. Fossen then frogmarched the man to the table, pulled his arms up over the back of one of the chairs, and pushed him roughly to sit down. He then threw a bundle of straps to Jules and told him to secure his victim's arms and legs to the chair."

"Whilst Jules was engaged in this, Fossen donned an apron and started chopping up some onions and tomatoes that he dug out from beneath the trolley. He lit the cooking ring, poured olive oil into a frying pan and started heating it on the hob. With the oil bubbling, he added the chopped vegetables and looked up to see that Jules had finished his task."

"Now you will undress please, Jules, and sit with your new friend", Fossen instructed him, and began to stir the mix slowly with a black plastic spatula from the barbeque set."

"Fearfully, Jules did as he was told. He had become accustomed to sexual play-acting over the time they had been partners. It had often been quite violent, and he began to pray that this one would not go too far."

"He was to be bitterly disappointed."

"It was a typically hot day in the Nevada desert, so it was not their nakedness that was causing both men to be shivering almost uncontrollably. After a short while, Fossen put down the spatula and calmly picked up one of the chef's knives.

Suddenly, he took a couple of paces towards Jules' lover, reached down between his legs and sliced off his penis. The room was immediately filled with screams from both men as Fossen calmly started to dice it up on the chopping block like a professional chef

- *slice slice slice slice* – just as he would a pepper or a German sausage. He then scooped it up on the knife and added it to the frying pan."

"The smell of cooking meat quickly filled the air as Fossen, almost as an afterthought, dived once more between the man's thighs. Swiftly, expertly, he winkled each testicle from their sack, chopped them in half and added them to the frying mix. It may have been the noise of all the screaming, which had now reached new levels, that seemed to change Fossen's mood. He was losing much of his calm now. He started muttering as he stirred more and more vigorously."

"OK, you motherfucker," he spat. "Now you're gonna feast on yourself, you fucking whore."

By now he was foaming at the mouth, every word being accompanied by a shower of spittle. He scooped up a spoonful of the genital fricassee. Every time the man opened his mouth to scream, Fossen forced in another spoonful, all the time shouting obscenities at him. The poor man tried not to swallow, but did so involuntarily as he was forced to take in air to breath."

"He was now leaking huge amounts of blood and was gradually losing consciousness. His screams became weaker and weaker. His jaw dropped and he began to swallow more and more of the foul meal. Fossen continued to force it in until the man finally slumped in his chair and ceased to offer any further resistance."

"Fossen was still raging, covered in blood and sweat - a terrifying sight. He spat in contempt at the body and turned to Jules. Whether he felt it was now to be his turn, or simply the horrifying spectacle he had just witnessed, he too had lost all the blood from his face and was heading into unconsciousness. He slipped off his chair and hit his head first on the edge of the table, then hard onto the stone floor."

"He remembered nothing more until he came to in near darkness. He was still naked, lying head first on some sort of couch. His head hammered and his body ached all over. As he sought to move himself off the couch, he felt sharp pains in and around his loins, and he realised that he had been violently raped as he had lain there. He felt a great tiredness coming over him again, and he submitted to it."

"He awoke again in the early morning. Stiffly, he managed to stand upright and look around him. He was on a small mezzanine floor over the diner. He looked for his clothes but could see no sign of them. As he went down the open staircase, he could see the whole of the diner, where there were no signs of the previous night's horrors. All the food had been thrown away and the blood and washed clean. The table, chairs and other props had all been cleared away, but there was still no trace of his clothes."

"He looked around the other buildings that made up the site. In one of them, he found a pair of old denim – how do you say, kombinezon."

"Overalls," suggested Tatyana, still looking very pale.

"Thank you. Yes - overalls. They were hanging amongst some bridles and harnesses. They were much too big for his slim frame, but he managed to wrap them close to him with the aid of some cord hanging from one of the windows. He could find no shoes, but he knew that the sand would not be too hot yet, and set out on the painful journey along the rough track that led to the highway."

"Miraculously, a car did eventually stop to give a lift to this sorry sight, and he soon found himself back in Vegas. He never saw Fossen again, but he was elated that he had somehow managed to survive. A friend gave him shelter where he was able to clean up and recover. Later, the same friend helped him to return to France and Paris where, several years later, he recounted the whole episode to Mussorgsky's friend."

Rubeliev paused, and then got up saying, "I'm sorry Mrs Fletcher."

Harry turned to look at Tatyana. She was white as a sheet, but from her colourless lips came, "Ugh... What a horrible man."

"Yes. He is." Rubeliev spoke theatrically, "Who will rid me of this troublesome beast?"

They looked at him silently, bemused.

His English classics studies unappreciated, Rubeliev continued, "Never mind. It's over to you now, Fletcher. It's not a case of - tit for tat, I believe is your expression. Not simply a matter of revenge. I doubt if many people will waste any tears on his demise."

He paused for tacit agreement, and then continued, "I'll print off some of the information we have on him, and get it to you at your hotel by noon today."

Harry looked at his watch which showed just after eight thirty. He looked at Rubeliev and asked, "It's morning then?"

"Yes. It's morning, Fletcher. You haven't been our guests for very long."

He stood up. "Now," he began. "If you're successful, I daresay you'll want to be paid for this contract. We'll need to agree a fund transfer method, so I'll need some bank details from you. We won't be meeting again once you leave this building today." He walked over to his desk, took out a small notebook from the centre drawer and looked up with pen poised.

Harry looked back at him. "I'm sorry," he said. "I don't have the necessary information. I'll get it to you later. Can I telephone you from the hotel?"

Rubeliev took out a card from his wallet and handed it to Harry. "Use this number. It's a secure private line and will always get through to me wherever I am - here and or my home. Use it to let me know of your progress too, please. Now, I have a busy day coming up. Have you any other questions before you leave?"

Harry looked at Tatyana and then shook his head. Rubeliev reached into a drawer and pressed a button. He led them to a door that had opened behind him and pointed. "There's your car", he said. "The key's in the ignition. As you know, we've removed a couple of items, but otherwise it's just as you left it." Then, after a pause, he smiled and added, "I believe you know where you are. I expect you know the way to your hotel?" Harry smiled sheepishly and nodded his head. They shook hands once more and Rubeliev indicated to the gatekeeper to open the outside doors.

Less than half an hour later, they were back in their room, finding it difficult to believe they had left it only some twelve hours earlier. Harry's first telephone call secured a couple of seats on an early evening flight back to London. He then telephoned Rubeliev and agreed a method of payment, and asked him if he could get the information on Fossen to the hotel as soon as possible.

They had a full and long breakfast, packed and settled the bill, then waited in the bar with a couple of drinks for Rubeliev's note.

By the time they landed at Heathrow, it had begun to drizzle lightly and they were pleased that the Audi was there to take them home. They were both physically and mentally exhausted, but went happily to bed early after a drink and a bite to eat.

It was not until the following morning that reality kicked in, and Harry began to consider the difficulties and dangers of the task that now loomed before him.

Chapter 16

However late he had gone to bed the previous night, Carl Fossen was always awake by 6.30 am. He spent the next half hour tuning his body for the day ahead in his own mini gym, twenty minutes on an exercise cycle and ten minutes with the weights. After a shower, he would dress and go down to the ground floor restaurant by 7.30 am. His breakfast would be waiting for him and was the same every day. He would start with a grapefruit, cut into halves. Then an oversize cup of black coffee would arrive before his main course – a skillet filled with crisp bacon, pork sausage, diced ham and onions, finally covered with melted cheese and two over-easy eggs. Unless he had a lunch appointment, perhaps a sandwich around midday would then last him until dinner.

By 8.30 am he would be behind his desk in his large top-floor office in the VCC building on Frank Sinatra Drive. Except for emergencies, he would have no meetings before 10.00 am. This time was taken up analysing the previous day's takings from the various casinos owned or managed by the Organisation. Each morning, he also received reports from all Casino Managers that had to be read, and actions taken where problems had been identified. Then there were all sorts of printed and video media extracts affecting the company and the industry in general. In addition to these, confidential and normally delivered by special couriers, were reports from home and abroad from Mafia-related organisations and individuals.

This particular morning, Fossen was most interested in the latter. He had received only very skimpy reports of Harry Fletcher's activities, but each morning he arrived at his office hoping to read the news of the sad demise of Viktor Rubeliev. Was this to be the morning? It would certainly add spice to his meeting later with Joe Becker.

But there was no such report. The only scrap of news from Russia was of a mysterious intrusion into a building site next door to the Rubeliev home. Whether or not this had any bearing on the contract was unclear, but certainly there were no reports of any deaths. Disappointed, Fossen reverted to his pile of overnight casino reports.

At 11.40 his secretary buzzed to let him know that Joe Becker had arrived. He was ten minutes late, and this called for punishment in kind. Fossen left him kicking his heels in his outer office whilst he finished signing off the previous night's takings. Just before the hour, flanked by an apologetic secretary, Joe forced his way into the room saying, "Come on, Carl. I'm only here for the day. I've got a lot of fucking work to get through."

Without standing up, Fossen waved his secretary out of the room and Becker to a chair in front of his desk. Although neither of them would ever admit it, the two had much in common. They never stood on ceremony, and neither had they any family to ask about the health of, so it was always straight down to business. The only big difference between them was that Fossen spoke very little, and when he did so it was with a degree of forethought. On this occasion, however, it was he who spoke first with a dry, "What can I do for you, Joe?" The use of his first name was as much familiarity as either could expect.

"Need yer help, Carl? Giovanni came by the other day and told me about yer plan for this fucking Ruskie. It's a dangerous move, I know, but it could work. He tells me you've got an experienced guy on the job, but it's not going to be easy for him. And there ain't much fucking time. Anyway, good luck to him."

"But what if he doesn't succeed?" Becker paused briefly, confused, "I don't know. I can't sleep at night. This guy's still gaining support, and I can't fucking well understand it."

"And if your man does succeed. What then? It'll be just Giovanni and me. I've got loads of support, but Giovanni's got the family thing. Why is he standing, Carl? He's too fucking old for one thing. I know you're working with him. Can't you get him to see sense and stand down?"

"No, Joe. If it turns out to be a straight fight between the two of you, I'll be supporting Giovanni every time."

"Aw, come on Carl. You can't be fucking serious. He's had his day. He's well past it..."

He seemed to go into a short reverie as Fossen kept silent. Then he started on a new tack. "Can't we come to some arrangement, Carl? What would you like? I mean, if we could somehow arrange for the field to open for me?"

"No deal, Joe. "I'd much prefer it if you were the one to drop out."

"No fucking way," Becker spat out immediately. "I was in the frame first, and I command more votes. If you're not gonna fucking help, I reckon I'll have to speak again to Giovanni."

"Do that," challenged Fossen. "He should be at home in LA. But I doubt if you'll get much joy though."

Becker pushed back his chair and got up. "Well I sure ain't quitting without a fucking fight," he said as he made for the door. "Bye Carl," he shouted over his shoulder and left with about as much grace as he had arrived.

Fossen thought for a while and then reached for the telephone. He decided that he had to report the meeting to Giovanni and warn him that Becker might be getting in touch with him. There was no reply from his home number, and he didn't wish to leave a message. He tried his cell phone and was just about to ring off when Giovanni answered in a quavering, uneven voice, "Carl," he said. "What's up?"

Fossen was momentarily thrown, concerned by Giovanni's unusual voice. "Are you OK, Giovanni?" he asked.

"Sure," Giovanni assured him. "I'm on the slab - having a massage. Hang on a sec." The line went quiet, but Fossen could just make out Giovanni, "Easy Mattie. Let me take this call. Come back in five minutes, eh."

"OK. I'm back with you." His voice had returned to normal. "What's up, Carl?"

"Joe Becker called in today. He wants you to stand down."

"Oh, God! Not again," Giovanni said wearily. "What did you say?"

"Same as we agreed. You're family – it's your duty. I suggested he was the one who should stand down, but he didn't like that. I thought I should warn you he's likely to get in touch with you again."

"Ok. Thanks. I know what to say to the little runt." He rolled over on his back. "Our contract with Harry Fletcher - have you heard anything?"

"Over the weekend, there was a break-in of some sort in a building site next to Rubeliev's house. Nothing more, so I don't know as it has anything to do with Fletcher. You?"

"No. Nothing. Keep in touch. Bye, Carl." He thumbed the phone off, and then, at the top of his voice he shouted, "Mattie."

Reinvigorated, Giovanni drove back to his home in Beverly Hills. He was greeted by his wife and two faithful Labradors. After a light lunch, uninteresting fare to conform to his doctor's orders, he set to on the telephone with the tiresome task of making call after call to solicit more support.

Giovanni had been married to Martha for over 40 years. In a way, they had remained remarkably faithful to each other throughout all these years. That is not to say that they had not engaged in extra-marital affairs - they both had. But they had remained together, tolerant and best friends.

He was not concerned about Joe Becker. He could always deal with him if he did phone. But he was getting nervous about his contract with Harry, who had always kept him well informed of progress in the past. Did the current silence mean that he was making no headway, was he perhaps in trouble, or was it simply that lines of communication from Russia were difficult?

He was pondering this, and wondering how he could get in touch when the telephone rang. It was the Director of the Sunset Hospice, and from the tone of his voice, Giovanni realised immediately that there was some bad news about his brother and it turned out to be the worst possible news. Rico's condition had worsened very suddenly during the morning and he had passed away just before midday.

The usual pointless questions immediately started swimming around in his mind. Why had he not visited Rico yesterday evening, as he had planned? What were his last words to him? He found it difficult to speak at first, but eventually managed to arrange a meeting with the Director at 3.00 pm. He wanted some time to compose himself before breaking the news to Martha, who was so very fond of his brother.

Giovanni walked over to the sideboard and took a printed family photo album from the right-hand drawer. He took it over to the sofa and sat quietly for a while, the book unopened on his lap, thinking of some of the moments when Rico had touched his life. Then he opened the book to the early years – happy, carefree days when his responsibilities seemed to begin and end with looking after his kid brother.

But suddenly, as he turned the pages, the guilt welled up again. There were almost no photos of Rico, nor even the rest of the family, for the period when he was in his late teens and twenties. He felt a punch in his stomach as recalled how he had neglected them all. He had left the family home and spent the next decade or so making his way in the Firm by day and playing fast and loose with a whole string of women after hours.

He realised now how much Rico must have missed the attention and companionship of his elder brother. He found himself wondering if this rejection and neglect had in some way affected his sexual orientation. Immediately, he tried to thrust all thoughts on that subject from his mind.

But he could not do so, and his thoughts turned to the dossier Fossen had given him. He had destroyed the DVD and burned the remainder of the file but, although it had sickened him to do so, he had read through the contents and was aware that the original was waiting somewhere to be released with the death of Fossen. Maybe he should call Fossen's bluff, now that Rico could no longer be hurt by the revelation. But almost immediately, he realised that it was just as important to him that Rico's memory remained untouched. He could not bear the thought of the effect it might have on Jackie and the children.

Returning to the album, his spirits were lifted by the later years - by the many happy photos and memories of their two families. Against all the odds, Jackie had turned out to be a splendid partner for Rico and a conscientious and inventive mother for their kids. They had all got on so well, meeting up most weeks, and rarely would a month go by without a weekend being spent together, either on the boat or at one of their houses in the country. The last several months had been extremely difficult, of course, and he found it almost impossible to believe that he would never again see that easy smile as Rico strode to meet them.

Martha had already steeled herself to the inevitable and was able to compose herself sufficiently to travel with him to the Hospice. They said their goodbyes to Rico, spending some time sitting by his still body, holding hands. It was the end of an era.

The director had arranged for the Undertaker to be present, and they discussed preliminary arrangements for the funeral, agreeing that it should be some time in the coming week.

When they returned home there was a message on the phone that Harry Fletcher had phoned, and Giovanni was somewhat alarmed to see that the number he gave for a return call was his London number. He called it immediately, eager to find out what was happening.

Harry was in a deep sleep when the telephone beside their bed rang, and it was some moments before he was orientated enough to croak a husky, "Hello" into it.

"Hi, Harry. You sound a bit dozy. What's up?"

Harry looked briefly at the clock. "It's two o'clock in the morning for Christ's sake. I was asleep."

"Aw. It's Giovanni Pollini - from Los Angeles. I forgot. So sorry."

Harry decided he should take the call. "Listen, Giovanni. I'll take the call downstairs. Hang on for a couple of minutes will you."

"OK, Harry."

He walked swiftly to the bathroom and sloshed some cold water over his face. With it still dripping, he went downstairs and picked up the phone.

"Hi, Giovanni. That's better," he said. "How are things with you?"

"Not good, Harry. Martha and I just got back from saying goodbye to my brother, Rico. He passed away this morning."

"Oh Giovanni, I'm so sorry." But how would it affect their contract, he wondered? Was he already out of time? "I know it was expected, but it's always a shock, isn't it"

"Yup. He was a great guy, Harry. We're all going to miss him real bad"

They were silent then - a mark of respect. It was Harry who eventually broke it.

"I haven't got any better news for you either, I'm afraid, Giovanni." He left the disappointment hanging in the air for a few moments. Then he continued, "As you probably know, I've been in Moscow. But things didn't quite turn out as planned." He paused, and then continued, "We have to talk, Giovanni."

"I haven't heard anything from my contacts out there, Harry. I take it Rubeliev is still alive and kicking."

"Yes," Harry confirmed. "It's a complicated story, but I can't report over the phone. I'm coming over." Then, he had an idea and started again, "Giovanni, I never met Rico but I'd like to be at his funeral if that's OK with you."

"Sure, Harry. We're trying to arrange it for next Sunday. It'll be quite a big do. There's going to be a whole bunch of people, but I'll be sure to get you an invite. I can't offer to put you up though. The house will be stuffed full of family. A mate of mine has a very nice small hotel not far from the church. I'll book you a room 'cos there'll sure to be a run on them. Just let me know when you're arriving. OK?"

"That's still a week away, Giovanni. I need to speak to you before then." Harry thought for a while and then said, "I'll come over in a couple of days, say - Wednesday. I'll give you a ring when I get in."

"OK, Harry. I'll email the hotel details to you. See you soon then. Back to sleep, Harry. Bye..."

Tatyana was still asleep as Harry slid gently in between the sheets. He lay there for a while thinking of the coming meeting with Giovanni. He couldn't tell him of his change of target. He had certainly detected that was no love lost between Giovanni and Carl Fossen, but they were, after all, running mates in the forthcoming contest.

His mind then turned to Rubeliev's theory that Fossen had some dirt on Giovanni and was blackmailing him. If it were true, would Fossen's death trigger some terrible revelation that would embarrass Giovanni? Somehow, he must try to discover if it was blackmail and, if so, the nature of it. And he would need to answer this before he could turn his mind to the main reason for his trip to the States - to the execution of his contract with Rubeliev.

Chapter 17

By the time Harry had passed through the lengthy US immigration process and was settled in his hotel, he felt it was too late to visit Giovanni. He telephoned him, only to find that he was out anyway, so he left a message that he had arrived.

He had always disliked the idea of eating in hotel restaurants. They were generally rather cold, impersonal places. So he left the hotel and wandered around the surrounding streets. It was largely a residential area, but he eventually came across an Italian pizzeria and decided to settle for that.

It had been tough leaving Tatyana. Indeed, the whole time since they had returned from Russia had been difficult for both of them. After the initial euphoria of getting back to England alive, the difficulties and dangers that faced Harry came to the forefront of both their minds. Tatyana eventually resigned herself to Harry finishing the job in America, and he had no concern that she might try to pull the same sort of stunt on the plane. She could be of no help with the language, and she still felt she had been something of a liability in the chase.

But she had not taken it well. She insisted that she would much prefer to have him at home - poor but alive - than rich, retired and dead. Harry had to remind her that it was not as simple as that. Rubeliev had made it quite clear that their release depended on the execution of the revised contract. Failure would mean a third contract – the two of them!

Over his pizza, Harry's mind turned to his forthcoming meeting with Giovanni, but there were too many imponderables and he left the restaurant none the wiser.

Entering his room, a light was flashing on the telephone beside the bed. It turned out to be a message from Giovanni. He apologised for not coming over to the hotel, but he was up to his eyes with arrangements for Rico's funeral. Could Harry come over to his house at around 10.30 am the next day?

He had turned up the air conditioning when he went out, but the room was still too hot for his English sensibilities and he spent a somewhat turbulent night, still trying to figure out the best line to take with Giovanni. For one thing, he did not know how much Giovanni knew of his adventures in Moscow. He would have to recount his efforts to assassinate Rubeliev in some detail but, when it came to that final evening, he would simply tell him that they had managed to escape in the Moscow Metro, and then returned immediately to England.

The ten hour flight the previous day, coupled with his restless night, left him in a poor mood for breakfast. He ordered a taxi at the front desk for 10.00 am and went for a short stroll to try to clear his head.

He had never visited Giovanni in his lair before and was impressed by the Beverly Hills pile that his cab pulled into. The gatehouse alone appeared to be as large as his own house back in England. A uniformed guard emerged, ordered the cab to move off, and escorted him inside. His name was checked against a list and he was searched thoroughly before being passed on to a suited guide who escorted them through immaculate gardens to the splendid mansion. The door was opened by another suit but it was Martha, Giovanni's wife, who advanced to greet Harry. They had met briefly only once, in London, but she knew that she owed her husband's life to this tall dark Englishman. As she led him through to Giovanni's study, she said, "I know how much he's looking forward to seeing you, Harry. If he seems a bit distracted, it's not you. At the moment, his mind is always half on things he might have forgotten for the funeral."

"Don't worry," replied Harry. "I won't keep him too long."

Giovanni rose from his desk as they entered. His face cracked open in a huge smile and, "Harry, il mio amico." Then he stepped forward with his arms open wide for a signature bear hug.

"I'll leave you guys to talk." said Martha, and then as she reached the door, "Shall I organise some coffee?"

"Please, Martha. Thanks," said Giovanni.

"You look tired, Harry. It's a long flight, eh."

"Yes," agreed Harry, "and I'm afraid I didn't have a very good night last night. Too hot..."

"The hotel not good?" asked Giovanni.

"No. No. It's fine, Giovanni. Many thanks. It's me. I'm just not used to the heat out here. I'm good."

"Now Harry. I wanna hear all about your trip to Russia. I did get a few bits and pieces of info. It was you who broke into the site next to Rubeliev's house, wasn't it?"

"Yup." Harry confirmed, and he spent the next twenty minutes giving Giovanni a detailed account of his efforts to fulfil their contract. After all, Giovanni had paid a considerable amount for them. If he remained unsuccessful, he didn't expect to be forced to refund the advance. That was an acknowledgement of Harry's preparedness to take on the task in the first place and for his preparations and efforts to fulfil it. Harry had already decided not to claim for expenses - unless Giovanni brought the subject up.

A stylish black girl in a matching uniform came in with the coffee and left quietly. Harry kept to his plan and explained how he and Tatyana had managed to jump on a train and escape home, unhurt and unexposed. Giovanni listened without interruption.

"You had some bad luck with those security guards, Harry," he said when Harry had finished. "On the other hand, you were fucking lucky to get away in time. I don't think you'd be here today if you hadn't."

"I guess you're right." Harry agreed, happy that Giovanni had appeared to accept his end to the report.

"Well, where do we go from here? I don't suppose you know this, Harry. It's more than a bit embarrassing actually, but Viktor Rubeliev is determined to attend the funeral on Sunday. In fact, he's already in the country."

Giovanni paused to watch Harry's reaction. Somewhere, perhaps in Fossen's dossier, Harry had read or heard that it was Riccardo and Viktor together who had forged the liaison between the American and Russian organisations. It was not surprising, therefore, that he would want to pay his final respects to his collaborator and friend. But this was all in hindsight. Harry simply hadn't anticipated it, and he was more than a little unnerved - shocked even.

Before Harry could respond Giovanni continued, "He's brought his wife with him too. And there's another man along as well – I don't know who he is."

Might he have brought his bodyguard, Harry wondered. Whatever the case, Harry realised that he would have to be careful, keep a very low profile - just observe. But again, Harry had been caught off guard. His anticipation seemed to have deserted him. "What. He's here?" Was all he could say limply,

"Well, don't you go thinking about taking him out here, Harry?" Giovanni said earnestly. "Whatever he's made of your efforts in Moscow, he doesn't seem to be over-concerned about coming to the States. I suspect it's largely because he's asked us to take care of his safety while he's here. That's quite usual, of course, but it's put me in the weird position of organising elaborate security arrangements for a man I want dead."

Giovanni could see Harry's surprise, and paused for a while before continuing, "Trouble is, Harry, time's running out rapidly - and he's still in the lead."

"It's a problem, Giovanni. But he has to be safe while he's here." Giovanni nodded.

Harry's mind was racing but in fact, all this appeared to take some pressure off him. With no need to worry about the first contract, it left him free to concentrate on the second. All those waking hours planning for this meeting seemed to have gone out of the window and, to give himself more time to think, he decided to start on another tack.

"Giovanni, how serious are you about this job? When we met in Naples, I came away with the impression that your heart wasn't really in it. You seemed somewhat - I don't know - disillusioned about it all; you wanted more time to enjoy life. Was I wrong?"

It was now Giovanni's turn to be wrong-footed, and it was clear on his face. The moment he spotted it, Harry decided to push home his advantage, "So why, Giovanni?"

"Well, Harry, it's a family thing. Six generations of Pollinis. I can't just let it go without a fight. And I would like the job to go to an American. That's sure important to me too."

"Oh. Come on, Giovanni. There must be more to it than that. You're prepared to kill for Christ's sake!"

Giovanni thought for a moment and then said rather limply, "Well, you asked the question, Harry. I've given you my answer."

"Sorry," said Harry. "I just don't get it. There has to be more to it than that."

Again, Giovanni did not answer, but simply shrugged his shoulders.

"I've got a theory," said Harry. He was about to hijack Rubeliev's ideas, but he would need to change some of the elements. "I've heard some pretty weird things about the man who was with you when we met in Naples – your running mate – Carl Fossen. He sounds a bit, shall we say, over-ambitious. A real hard man, eh."

Again, Giovanni said nothing, but just pursed his lips and stared at Harry with his head cocked to one side.

"So," Harry continued, "I figure he might have put you up to it. But why do you go along with it? That's my problem. He's got to have some sort of hold over you."

Harry waited for a reaction from Giovanni, who remained silent. He decided on a full frontal attack then, and continued, "I'm told he has a history of blackmailing – even his own men. Has he got something on you, Giovanni? Is he blackmailing you?"

Oddly, the form of this direct question gave Giovanni an honest escape route. He was able to say, "You've got it all wrong, my friend. He's got nothing on me. Straight up, Harry, I'm squeaky clean. He couldn't have anything."

Harry looked at his friend for a while. The way he'd couched his reply left him with nagging doubts, but he managed to suborn them for the moment. "I'm sorry, Giovanni. I had to know. Forgive me?" He held out his hand. Giovanni looked at it for a moment, then grabbed and shook it, "Sure, Harry. Sure."

Harry left soon afterwards, leaving Giovanni to get on with his funeral arrangements. But as he did so, his thoughts kept returning to the meeting. It had ruffled him. Had Harry believed him? And was Harry the only person to have reached the same conclusion? It was not long before the germ of an idea began to grow in his mind.

Systematically, he checked one more time through all the complex preparations he and Martha had made for Ricardo's funeral only three days hence.

When he had finished, he switched off his computer and made a sudden decision. He got up and went in search of Martha.

Within the hour, he was behind the wheel of his 2006 Aston Martin DB9 Volante driving east along Interstate 10. Giovanni had always enjoyed driving. Over recent years, Martha had frequently tried to persuade him to employ a chauffeur to drive him around, but he had so far managed to resist. However, as a small acknowledgement of his advancing years he had, about three years earlier and with great reluctance, finally parted with his beloved 1966 E-Type Jaguar.

The drive to Las Vegas was likely to take the best part of four hours, so he settled back listening to some jazz and rehearsing the conversation he was going to have with Carl Fossen. He had deliberated at some length whether or not to invite Carl to the funeral but had eventually decided that it would be somewhat churlish not to do so. They had, after all, shared several years of their past lives together. Carl had accepted, so would himself be travelling to LA in the next day or so. But Giovanni decided it couldn't wait. He would be far too busy during the coming days, and wanted to get the matter settled - one way or another.

Suspecting that Fossen's office and apartment would probably both be wired, he had arranged to meet him at 7.00 pm in one of the bars in the Venetian Hotel, where Giovanni had decided to stay for the night. If it was too busy to talk freely, they could always go up to his room.

He arrived in good time and booked into his favourite hotel on the Strip. He waived aside the management welcome that always greeted him, and settled into his suite. Just before time, he went down to the Double-Helix Bar where he found Fossen already seated in a quiet corner. As Giovanni approached, Fossen poured him a glass of Chardonnay from a bottle on the table.

"How are the preparations going?" he asked, with just a gentle nod for a greeting.

"Hey, Carl. OK, thanks. I'm sure I'll have forgotten something though. And you won't believe the cost of everything."

"So, what can I do for you, Giovanni?" It was so typical of Fossen - little greeting, no niceties, straight down to business. Giovanni smiled and decided on a more oblique approach.

"You know all three of us will be there, don't you?" he said, more a statement than a question.

"All three?" Fossen queried.

"The three front runners for Rico's job."

Fossen seemed surprised at the thought of Rubeliev being present, perhaps because he had already anticipated his demise. Or perhaps he considered Giovanni would find it difficult to invite a man whose death he had tried to arrange.

"No. I didn't. I'm surprised you sent Rubeliev an invite."

"I felt I had to, Carl. He and Rico had met many times and were good friends. It would have seemed very odd if I hadn't."

"Well, what's Fletcher doing?" Fossen asked. He sounded somewhat exasperated. "I haven't heard of any real solid attempt. Is he still trying or not?"

"As far as I know he's still onto it. I've spoken to him on the phone, and I know he's gotten close a couple of times." Giovanni had decided that he would not tell Fossen that Harry had left Russia, let alone the fact that he had met with him only a few hours ago just down the road, in Los Angeles.

"Well he ain't got much time now," Fossen said flatly.

There was silence then, as Giovanni searched for a suitable introduction to his ultimatum. In the end, he decided to go in head first.

"I've been thinking, Carl. As you know, I've never really wanted this job. I'd much prefer to take a back seat and enjoy the time that's left to me with my family. And anyway, I'm not at all sure I'm up to it..."

"I've told you, Giovanni," interrupted Fossen. "You don't have to worry about that. I'll be behind you all the way."

"I know, Carl. And don't think that fact doesn't worry me too," Giovanni said. He had promised himself that he would try not to get angry but, as usual when meeting Fossen, he was already beginning to feel irritated. He paused for a while, then cut straight to the bone, "Your threat - your fucking blackmail, don't mean too much now, Carl. With Rico dead, it ain't worth more than a hill of beans. So I intend to pull out of the race..."

Fossen's face remained expressionless, with no signs of anger or disappointment. But he did cut in quickly, "You can't mean that, Giovanni. You surely must value his memory - and his reputation."

"Yeah. I do. But I'm even more worried about the living - his wife and kids. How would it affect them?" He shook his head.

"And that's why I'm prepared to offer you a deal," he continued. "If you hand over the dossier held in the bank vault, along with everything else you may have squirrelled away, I'll agree to continue with our campaign. After all, I would prefer to see the job stay in the States."

Fossen was silent.

"You gonna have to make a quick decision, Carl." Giovanni insisted. "I'm scooting back to LA tomorrow morning - very early. And if I leave without every single thing you've got on my brother, then I'm going to announce immediately, before Rico's funeral, that I'm no longer in the running."

Fossen remained silent for only a short time before he asked "How do I know you'll keep your part of the bargain? Once you've got the stuff, you could just walk away"

"Honour amongst thieves, Carl. How can I be sure that you have given me everything?" And after a pause, he added "Do you suppose that if either of us screwed up, he would have much of a future on this Earth? I certainly have no illusions about the actions you would take."

Again Fossen had to think, but for only a short time before he agreed, "OK. But I've got some telephoning to do. The vault will be closed at this time.

I'm sure I can get access, but I've gotta get hold of someone. Are you gonna stay here?"

"I guess so," said Giovanni. "I'll finish up the wine - thank you. And I'll get something to eat from the bar. Don't be too long. I might be too drunk to remember what I've agreed to."

As Fossen got up he added, "And make sure you include everything mind". This thought set him worrying, and he continued, "Hey, wait a moment, Fossen. I don't fucking trust you. You arrange for access, and then pick me up. I'm coming with you. I don't want you copying anything."

Fossen shrugged, went to another part of the lounge and began telephoning. Giovanni refilled his glass and sauntered over to the bar to order a plate of Angus steak and blue cheese.

It was some time before Fossen returned, announcing that they would have to leave for the security vaults immediately, which obliged Giovanni to wolf down his food. When they arrived, the man who met them had also been eating and was picking remnants from his teeth. He knew Fossen well, chatting to him as he carried out a brief security check, and patted them both down in a very perfunctory manner.

He left Fossen and Giovanni with an armed security guard in a small room containing just a table and chairs, then emerged from the vault after a couple of minutes with a steel box and placed it on the table in front of Fossen. After re-setting the vault security, both he and the guard left the room.

Fossen opened the deposit box, took out a file and handed it to Giovanni who immediately recognised its red cover. He briefly examined the contents. Apart from the 'IN CASE OF OWNER'S DEATH' instructions pinned to the front cover, it appeared to be identical to the copy he had already destroyed. After quickly flipping through to check that the DVD and other major elements were present, he nodded to Fossen and tucked it under his arm. Before the box was closed, he noticed that there were numerous other files in a variety of colours. Fossen closed up the box and pressed the bell to announce that they had finished.

Giovanni returned to the Venetian, well satisfied with his night's work, and ready to face a gruelling weekend.

Chapter 18

Henry and Roland got their early morning call just as the first signs of another glorious Californian day began to paint a glimmer of light onto the night sky. Their grooms opened the large stable doors and rustled some straw into their stalls. Whilst the two handsome black dray horses ate their morning snack, the men busied themselves unhooking and taking into the yard the various items of tack that would be required for the day.

Each horse was led into the yard, exercised for around ten minutes, and groomed thoroughly for the day's performance. They were large animals and were bundled into their horsebox for transportation to the Funeral Director's collecting enclosure in the City. This then became a procession when a third transporter carrying the black Marsden hearse joined them for the journey, by now in full daylight.

Waking about twenty minutes later than these beasts, Fernando eased himself out of his bunk bed, trying in vain to rub the previous night's alcoholic sleep from his eyes. He thumped the top of his alarm clock to silence the increasingly insistent din. Still only in his boxer shorts, he was whistled at by a couple of smartly uniformed waitresses as he padded to the washroom for his morning ablutions.

Once dressed in his crisply laundered white gear, he made his way along the underground corridors to the kitchens of the Westin Bonaventure Hotel. Among cries of "Morning Ferdo" he arrived at his station only to find the morning shift's Head Chef already frying some eggs.

"Come on, Fernando," he shouted at him. "Get cracking. The rush has already started. Here, grab this list."

Over the next four hours, he would fry some two thousand eggs on his griddle, all to order – hard, over medium, over easy, sunny side up. He soon began to look forward to his first cigarette of the day at 10.30 am.

Helen Brophy was woken nearly an hour later than Fernando by her mother, who was just off to the local Primary school where she did her best to implant some enthusiasm for learning into her seven and eight-year-olds. Her daughter had asked to be woken early as she was needed at Conroy's Flowers to finish off the preparations for a large funeral contract.

She had a ten minute walk from where the bus dropped her off and spent the time wondering if the boy she had met the previous evening would be interested enough to telephone. She quite fancied him.

Once inside the workshop, there was no time for such idle thoughts. She was fully engaged in fashioning the wreaths and other floral tributes that would be taken to the church, to the reception, or to the morticians to accompany the coffin. She was good at this, and worked swiftly, aware that she was appreciated by her boss.

Giovanni too had woken early, for he had much to do today. For a start, he wanted to give his eulogy one last look. He eased himself out of bed without waking Martha and went downstairs to his study. When he had finished, he gave it a satisfied nod and carefully placed it alongside all the other bits and pieces he would need to squirrel away in the black suit that he had selected to wear. By this time, he could hear the household gradually coming to life. He had arranged for extra kitchen staff to arrive early and, whilst not on the same scale as Fernando, the smell of eggs frying told him that breakfast was on its way.

At about the same time, Viktor Rubeliev was just about to start tucking into a couple of Fernando's eggs in his downtown hotel. His wife, Elena, had ordered some yoghurt and fruit, but they had yet to appear. They had arrived in Los Angeles a couple of days earlier and, at Elena's insistence, they had set about enjoying all the standard local tourist attractions.

At Universal Studios, they had enjoyed visiting Bates Motel, the site of one of Elena's favourite films, and were thrilled to the Jurassic Park ride. In a more serious vein, whilst Viktor attended a couple of meetings he had organised, Elena had immersed herself in the arts at the Getty Centre and City Museum. But today was going to belong to Riccardo Pollini.

It is perhaps as well that Carl Fossen and Joe Becker had chosen to stay in different downtown hotels. And it was from the whole gamut of Los Angeles hotels that mourners from all corners of the globe emerged in black suits or dresses and began to converge on the Catholic Church at the corner of W 3rd Street and S Van Ness Avenue.

On the previous evening, Giovanni had telephoned Harry at his hotel. He was concerned that he might run into Carl Fossen at the funeral as he had just implied to him that Harry was still in Russia. Somewhat unnecessarily, he also reminded him that there was to be no attempt to fulfil the contract on American soil.

Harry too had become somewhat uneasy about his presence at the funeral and offered to stay away. However, it was eventually agreed that he should arrive early and Giovanni would arrange for a seat for him in a discreet area.

The church was only a short walk from Harry's hotel, but he found that there was already a queue at the doors where tickets were being examined. He was shown to a staircase at the side and to a seat in the front of the choir loft, which was acting today as an overflow. It was to be more than half an hour before the whole church was filled and cameras were finally positioned for a closed circuit relay to a second congregation at the reception venue a couple of miles away.

Henry and Roland had been tethered to the matching black hearse and were now trundling slowly along the length of Van Ness Avenue carrying Riccardo's coffin, festooned with flowers. Walking behind them were the chief mourners, the family and closest friends. The street was lined with many other friends and colleagues who had not got tickets to the church and would be going straight on to the reception. As the procession approached the church, the choir, which had been evicted from their usual loft, entered and arranged themselves quietly in two deep semi-circles in front of the altar and behind the presiding priest. All was set.

The coffin arrived inside, carried by eight bearers, including one of Riccardo's sons. It was placed on its trestle, shrouded in purple satin. Rico's widow, Jackie, and their children sat down in the left-hand front row, and when the second row had filled up with other family members, the big doors were closed.

Whilst Harry was mouthing the opening hymn, silently as he did not wish to inflict his unpleasant singing voice on others, he was able to pick out the various protagonists seated below him. Giovanni was seated with Martha and the family on the right hand side of the front row. Four rows back on the same side sat Viktor Rubeliev with his wife and Vladimir Mussorgsky, who Viktor had brought along for company and probably a degree of protection. Six rows behind them, on the other side were Joe Becker, along with a number of his lieutenants from Chicago. Leaning forward, Harry could just make out the top of Carl Fossen's head, who was seated almost underneath him with a couple of his men from Las Vegas. He wondered what thoughts were going through each of their heads.

As the service progressed, Giovanni gave his brother a noble send-off in his eulogy. He recalled the early days when, with both parents occupied on most days, his younger brother was frequently placed into his care. He loved his kid brother and made it his duty to protect him.

He recounted one episode, however, where he and his gang had somewhat recklessly used him as bait in one of their very first scams. Beyond the woods at the end of their garden, a footpath meandered alongside a small stream. During the summer holidays,

Giovanni and his gang of five would spend many long hours here, playing a variety of games which often involved cops and, increasingly often, robbers. Over time, they developed many ways of augmenting their pocket money. It was something in the blood.

The footpath which ran between the Maryland Estate and the main road provided access to a small collection of local shops, as well as public transport to local schools and further afield. It was well frequented in those days when the car was not used for every journey. The gang would watch from the top of a bank which ran above the path and pick their victim carefully. Little Rico would then be despatched down to sit beside the path, crying his heart out.

His angel features and small, sobbing frame would quickly melt the heart of almost all their victims, who would run to him and bend down to find out what the problem was. Often, they would scoop Rico up in their arms. Between sobs, he would tell them that he was lost. The Good Samaritan would look around for help, which was the cue for a couple of the gang to run down to ask what was going on. They would give out a story of how they knew the toddler and where he lived, and could get him home on the bus – but they did not have any money for the fare. Most times they would be handed money for all of their fares, and quite frequently some extra for ice cream at the corner shop.

After some success, they decided to up the ante. They had found they could get more money if they spun a little hard luck story about Rico or his parents. On one day, however, their enthusiasm for money exceeded their prudence. With their saddest faces on display, they explained to a plain-clothed policewoman, who had been charged with investigating complaints against them, that the poor boy had just been orphaned - his parents having been attacked and killed by a pack of wild dogs.

When the nervous laughter from the congregation had subsided Giovanni continued, "We were given a strong warning by the policewoman and marched home to my parents. I got a walloping from my Dad - but only half-hearted, 'cos I think he appreciated our enterprise. In fact, it was soon after this that he started training me up for our profession."

This produced some more uneasy laughter, and Giovanni continued with an alternate mixture of amusing and more serious recollections. The service proceeded in the usual form of Requiem Mass and included some quiet time for each of them to recall his or her memories of Ricardo.

Eventually, the whole congregation joined with the overflow at the reception. Giovanni had catered for some five hundred people, but it was likely to be considerably more.

Harry had almost decided not to attend in case he ran into Carl Fossen, but he did wish to say farewell to Giovanni before he left for Las Vegas. Initially, he also thought it might present an opportunity to fulfil his new contract with Fossen outside the comfort zone of his home territory, but he soon discarded the idea. Very early on, he saw how the place was bristling his Fossen's men and indeed, the whole place was alive with bodyguards and villains of all sorts. But if he did run into Fossen, he decided he would confide, perhaps with a wink, that he was chasing some unfinished business left over from Moscow.

There was no formal dining. The place was enormous and people mingled throughout one vast hall and several smaller rooms, picking up buffet food and drinking champagne.

It was not long before Carl Fossen, who intensely disliked such affairs, felt that he had stayed for a sufficiently respectful time and rounded up his men, preparing to leave. On their way out he decided on a visit to the toilets on the balcony floor. When he emerged, he stopped for a while, looking down at the crowd below. Some were eating, others were just chatting, but all were drinking. It was a sea of black, but it was getting merrier and more raucous by the minute. This was a gathering of all sorts of tough men with differing loyalties. In Fossen's experience, it would not be long before scuffles would break out, quite probably followed by more serious mayhem. That decided him, and he turned to leave.

As he did so, he suddenly stopped in his tracks and moved back to the balcony with his eyes blinking and his mouth hanging open in surprise. On the far side of the room, he had spotted a man he recognised from Naples as Harry Fletcher. He had no idea that he might be present. He was surely in Moscow.

But if that was a surprise, an even greater one was to follow. Fletcher was smiling and talking to the man that they had hired him to kill - Viktor Rubeliev.

It was only for one brief moment, and then Fletcher leaned and whispered something in the Russian's ear. They both looked around them rather furtively, shook hands briefly and Rubeliev walked away to join a woman - presumably his wife. Fletcher sidled away too, continuing to look around to see whether they had been seen together. Fossen instinctively moved his body backwards and out of Fletcher's line of sight.

What the hell was going on? Why was Fletcher here? Why was he shaking hands and talking with the man he had been contracted to kill? How had the Russian come to know him at all? His mind was ablaze with the possibilities, and he did not like any of them.

He turned, nodded to his men, and they all left to return to their hotel. He had intended to stay for another night in LA, but he decided to return that very day to Vegas, and the security of his apartment. He needed time and space to think.

As he settled himself down on the back seat for the long drive, the scene he had witnessed played over and over in his mind. Until that morning, his intelligence had indicated that Fletcher and his wife had escaped after being chased from the restaurant. But a report had arrived from Moscow that very morning suggesting that Fletcher had almost certainly been captured by Rubeliev's men in the metro station. A number of men had been seen struggling out of the Metro with a man and a woman who appeared to be very much the worse for wear. They were bundled into a couple of cars, which then drove off at speed. If these two were indeed Fletcher and his wife, then why were they not dead? How had they escaped back to England? And what was he doing here now?

The most likely scenario, he finally decided, was some sort of deal being struck. With his wife captured alongside him, he would no doubt have been more open to persuasion through threats of physical harm to her.

He tried to put himself in Rubeliev's shoes. What would he do if he discovered that someone had ordered his assassination? His immediate thoughts would surely be of revenge, and what neater way than to persuade the assassin to switch his target? But who would that be – Giovanni or himself, perhaps both?

Maybe he was just being paranoid. Perhaps Fletcher was still trying to fulfil the contract and had simply followed his prey to LA. There could be any number of other explanations, but he decided that he should step up his security arrangements. One thing was certain - his worst fears would be confirmed if Fletcher should ever turn up in Las Vegas.

During his university years, Fossen had developed the habit of taking copious notes. There was little wrong with his memory, but he found it helped to organise both his mind and his work. From then on, he had been a compulsive list-maker and inveterate note-taker. He dug a roller pen and a pad from his briefcase and started to write down some thoughts.

He had already started a dossier on Fletcher, and he remembered that he had a photo on file given to him early on by Giovanni. Tomorrow, he must have it copied and circulated amongst all his people. He wanted to make sure that he would be the very next person to know if Fletcher were ever to hit town.

Next, he turned his attention to areas of vulnerability. At least until he was sure that Fletcher had left the country, he would beef up his security. He made a note to appoint a couple of security men to accompany him on all his journeys to and from work – indeed any time he was outside of his office or apartment. He was fairly confident about his time in the office where there was already excellent security, but he decided that the two men should remain stationed in the outer lobby of his room as added protection.

Finally, he wrote down "apartment". He thought for a while and then scrubbed through it. Security here was fine, he decided. It had been well covered many years earlier when the building had first been constructed.

It is quite difficult to count the floors of any tall building. By the time your eyes have got to about the tenth row of windows, you begin to lose confidence that you are not missing some, and you start all over again. But if you really wanted to know how many floors there were, why not simply ask at reception, or check the top floor number on the elevators?

But these methods too would fail with the Saloma Tower. An additional floor had been incorporated during its construction. In the chaos which is a building site, this was never challenged by the City's Building Control or Planning authorities. Either they had failed to spot the addition or, more likely, a number of greenbacks had changed hands.

Gamblers rely on luck, and virtually no building in Las Vegas contains a floor with the unlucky number thirteen. However, in Saloma Tower, anyone measuring the time between floors in the elevator might perceive a slightly longer gap between the twelfth and fourteenth floors, before it continued up to the penthouses on the twenty-fourth and final level. This gap secreted an entire floor lost to the rest of the world and consisted of several apartments for Mafia bosses whose activities are less reliant on luck. Some became their permanent addresses, whilst others were reserved for visiting associates. It was served by a dedicated lift that was operated from a manned lobby off the administration offices behind the Reception Desk. The lobby itself could only be accessed by special swipe cards.

Over the years, this accommodation had given rise to the local expression of being "called to the thirteenth". Such a summons meant one of two things. One could hope that a particularly good or brave piece of work had been noticed, and was due to be acknowledged in words, money or an elevation in status. Unfortunately, it was much more likely to be at the other end of the scale. Any misdemeanours raised the very real possibility of some terrible form of retribution. Only for very minor breaches would this be carried out within the building. More serious offenders would be frogmarched down in the elevator to a secluded section of the basement car park and then taken for a ride.

The destination for the vast majority of such rides would be the old ghost settlement known as McCauley's Rest. This was a small collection of buildings some two miles or so off State Highway 93. In a previous life, it had been a refuelling stop for both cars and humans along the old stagecoach route, now almost entirely lost to the wind-blown sands of the desert. It had been purchased many years earlier by Fossen's predecessor as a lonely site for interrogations, and for meting out beatings and executions.

This place, along with the secret floor in the Saloma Tower, had long been known by the Las Vegas Police Department, but they had chosen to turn a blind eye to both of them. For a start, it was none of their business if the Mob wished to mete out punishments and death to its own people. It was one fewer villain in circulation. And they were happy for the mobsters to remain under the impression that their comings and goings were hidden from them. It made monitoring them that much less complicated.

When Giovanni had recommended Harry Fletcher, he had described him as both resourceful and persistent. He would need to add a whole load of luck to get anywhere near to him in his home, Fossen decided, and he went to sleep that night confident of his safety.

Chapter 19

Harry had already tried to establish whether Fossen's assassination would have any repercussions for Giovanni. He felt he could do no more but, in any case, he had no option but to proceed with his contract with Rubeliev.

The information that the Russian had given him on Fossen had been very sketchy. Although he headed up the Las Vegas operations, this was one of the finest jewels in the Mob's crown and other bosses, including Giovanni, certainly influenced its various operations. The majority of Fossen's work revolved around gambling houses. It gave the address of his apartment in the Saloma Tower, located in a block behind the New York-New York hotel complex, and also listed a number of his known associates.

Harry felt unable to formulate any sort of plan without a thorough investigation on the ground. He had once before visited Las Vegas, but only as a tourist and his most vivid memory was how very crowded it was. Not for the first time, he wondered how he had got himself into this mess.

Over the last few days, he had begun to kick an idea around in his mind, one that kept returning whenever he considered the problem. He recalled the story that Rubeliev had recounted, and he could picture in his mind the lonely spot where it had taken place. How ironic it would be if he could somehow lure Fossen out there for a showdown, and it might also make his job easier - away from the crowds in the city.

He determined to reconnoitre the place as soon as he hit Las Vegas.

He decided to hire a car for the journey and, not having had an opportunity to see Giovanni at the funeral, he drove first to his house to say goodbye. Both Giovanni and Martha were in fine spirits. The pressures of the last few days were over, and all had gone smoothly. Giovanni did not ask about Harry's intentions. Maybe he felt it would be wiser to remain ignorant, or perhaps he did not wish to put him on the spot, since he had ducked the question earlier.

He did not stay long but, as he was leaving, he asked Giovanni if he knew of a collection of deserted buildings owned by the Mob somewhere outside Las Vegas.

Giovanni smiled and said, "What the hell do you want to know that for, Harry?"

"Just curiosity," Harry said. "I heard a weird story some time ago about a happening out there. It involved Carl Fossen I think."

"I reckon I can guess the one you mean, Harry." He paused for a while, smiling ruefully. Then he said, "It's called McCauley's Rest. It's a turn off the Highway along a dirt road. You'll find it on most maps. If you are thinking of looking for it though, you be careful, Harry. It's not on the usual tourist trail."

"Sure. I'll remember that. You say Rubeliev is staying in the States for a couple of days, so I thought I'd drive over to Las Vegas for a bit of relaxation before I get back to work – play a few cards, take in a show or two."

Once again, Harry felt a pang of conscience at lying to Giovanni, but there was no way he could take him fully into his confidence. He congratulated the two of them on all the great work they had put into Rico's funeral, said his goodbyes and left for Las Vegas. Somehow, he doubted whether they would ever meet again.

He arrived in the early evening and checked into the New York-New York Hotel, being nearest to Fossen's apartment.

The following morning he decided to ignore Giovanni's advice and drove out to have a look at McCauley's Rest. As he left the basement car park, he was immediately engulfed in The Strip's traffic and it took him more than twenty minutes to reach the comparative calm of US highway 93, heading west towards Mesquite. McCauley's Rest was listed on the navigation system, and he pulled over to set it as his destination.

When prompted, he turned off left onto a lumpy dirt road. At times, swirling sand made it difficult to see the right track. At other times, flash streams had left deep ruts that severely tested the car's springs. Harry began to wish he had rented an off-road vehicle rather than the Chevrolet sedan. He battled with this road for the best part of twenty minutes before a group of run-down buildings appeared in front of him. He parked in front of what he took to have once been the diner. The glass entrance door had long since been broken and replaced by a pair of crude wooden doors secured by a heavy-duty padlock. Harry wandered down the right-hand side and came across a broken window.

Somebody had already forced their way in, and he had no difficulty in following suit.

Hoisting himself in, Harry found himself at the end of a short corridor with doors ranged along either side. Ignoring these, the passage eventually led him into the diner where he could immediately envisage the scene Rubeliev had described. Walking across the floor, he even spotted a wooden trolley that could have held the cooking apparatus, along with several tables and chairs. He idly wondered if any of these had been used again since that event, and to what terrible purpose. When he reached the opposite end, a staircase led up to a half floor which looked down onto the diner through what was left of a broken set of bannisters. This contained a couple of ragged old sofas and a writing desk probably having once served as some sort of living room for the owners.

Harry left the diner through a rear door which had bolts top and bottom, but no other visible sort of lock. He promised himself he would return the same way and re-make the bolts before he left. Immediately, he found himself in a courtyard that had once been a livery area. Four or five stables were ranged on the far side and to the right a building which, when he entered it, turned out to be a forge. The furnace was still intact and, as he examined it, had been used in the not-too-distant past. He had no difficulty in guessing what it had been used for over those recent years. Human ashes scattered to the wind and sands of the desert would have no difficulty in hiding from even the most diligent of DNA investigations.

Harry wandered slowly around the forge, occasionally stopping to examine an item hanging from the walls. He arrived back at the furnace and opened the door. It was empty, swept of all ash and thoroughly cleaned.

He moved back to the door and took a couple of steps outside to gaze once more at the livery yard. Suddenly, right behind his left ear, he heard the unmistakable double *click* of a six-shooter being cocked.

Instinctively, he raised his hands, his body forming the traditional trident of surrender. A deep southern drawl uttered quietly, "Don't you move a muscle, son."

Harry felt his body being frisked all over. It was one of those thorough searches that infiltrated every corner and private crevice and took some little time. Eventually, the man continued, "OK, son. You can turn around, and lower your hands. But don't you try anything, y'hear? This trigger's the lightest one around these parts."

Harry slowly did as he was told. He was somewhat startled to find a man standing in front of him who matched most precisely the image suggested by his voice. He was a tall man, dressed entirely as a cowboy. Under his wide Stetson was a face of dry leather, the colour of the desert sand after rain and complete with its crags and crevices. "This here's private property," the man said. "What you doin' poking around it, son?"

"Sorry. I thought it was deserted," Harry said. He had gained a few seconds to consider his excuses.

"Look, I'm just an English tourist. We don't carry guns. I got tired of the crowds and glitzy life in Vegas and took to the road. I've always been interested in history, and wondered what this place was on the map. I've just been looking around."

He stretched out his hands at either side. "No harm done," he said. "I haven't taken anything." Then, after a short pause, and with a smile on his face, "What are you doing here then?"

The man thought for a few seconds, then seemed to accept this as a friendly advance. "I'm paid to look after the place," he said as he un-cocked the gun and twirled it back into the holster at his hip.

Harry looked around him. "Looks like you're falling down on the job," he said teasingly, pushing his luck a bit. The man said nothing but just stared back at Harry, either not understanding the remark, or simply choosing to ignore it.

"Where's your horse?" Harry asked, pushing the man further.

The cowboy nodded in the direction of the wreck of the old gas station. "Hitched up over there," he announced. "Now, are you finished up here? You seen all you want? 'Cos I'd sure appreciate it if you'd get in your car and hightail out 'a here pretty damned soon."

"OK," agreed Harry. "Do you mind if I just walk around the gas station - round the outside to where my car is?"

The man did not answer, but simply lifted his head slightly in the direction I'd suggested. Harry took this as permission and set off with a chirpy, "Bye. Thank you."

The cowboy, who had been leaning against the door frame, eased himself forward and started off to walk some six feet or so behind Harry, who heard him but resisted the urge to turn round. As he rounded the corner at the far side of the gas station, the man's steed was waiting patiently and quietly. Despite its age, Harry immediately recognised it as an Oldsmobile pickup truck. He half turned, smiled briefly and continued to his own car parked outside the diner.

The journey back to Vegas was equally slow, but the cowboy did not follow. Harry had no idea whether he had been there all the time, watching his every move, or whether he had arrived when he was inside the diner or forge. What he did realise, however, was that he would not now be able to use the place for killing Fossen. The man would be sure to report the incident, which might arouse some suspicion in Fossen. At this stage, of course, Harry was unaware that Fossen's mind was already awash with suspicions.

Before returning to his hotel, Harry decided to go on a short shopping spree. With time on his hands in Los Angeles, he'd done some research and he turned off the highway onto West Hacienda. Numerous gun shops are located in this area, and he knew that Vegas gun laws would allow him to arm himself with little of the hassle that he had experienced in Moscow.

In the first store, completing a simple form allowed him to purchase on his credit card a Beretta 92 semi-automatic, complete with an AAC noise suppressor. He started mumbling an explanation about target practice and minimising noise nuisance, but the storeowner showed only the very slightest interest as he completed the sale.

The salesman in the second store did ask more searching questions and wanted to make a POS background check, with the possibility of a 72-hour delay. However, when Harry produced his English passport and explained he would not be around in 72 hours, he shrugged and continued with the sale of a Smith & Wesson SD9 handgun, again on his credit card. Further along Hacienda, Harry bought a medium size hunting knife from a sporting goods store.

Back in his hotel room in Vegas, he considered his rather limited options. Unknown to him, Carl Fossen had already received notification from the front desk at New York-New York that Harry Fletcher had arrived in Vegas, and was at the very same moment considering his own options.

The die had been cast. Each man was moving inexorably along his road towards the OK Corral.

Chapter 20

The role of an assassin is not for everyone. It takes a very particular sort of person. There are those who, for one reason or another, take a dislike to all forms of humanity, cut themselves off from normal society and live their lives in the shadows. A small proportion of these will end up as murderers, but none will have either the contacts or discipline to make an assassin. At the other end of the spectrum, many more people would never even utter a bad word against their fellow man, let alone do him any physical harm.

In between, there are certain ordinary individuals, like Harry, who meet with an episode in their lives that changes some of their normal attitudes to violence. The vast majority of such events stem from one or other form of military service, giving them the necessary discipline, knowledge and experience. And many of these will have had the experience of making a legal kill.

The job presents many unique problems. For a start, the quarry is frequently a man of violence, which makes him a dangerous adversary. And he may well anticipate the danger, prompting him to erect a wall of defensive measures. This leads to the greatest problem for all assassins – how to get close enough to their victim to make the kill without jeopardising their own safety and means of escape.

Every job ends with the kill itself - the hit. Each assassin will have his own set of favourite techniques. Some will have a whole arsenal to call on. Harry had been taught to rely on simplicity, ignoring such exotic methods as poison gas spray guns, polonium ingestion poisoning, and the like. He stuck to what he knew, what he had been trained in using – rifles, handguns, and knives.

The kill itself requires a strong stomach and Harry, like many others, always sought to justify to himself the need for his action. He would never be able to kill a child and, fortunately for him, he had never been asked to assassinate a woman. He had often wondered what his response would be to such a request. But he had no such doubts about the kill that he now faced. He personally disliked the man, and he knew that even Fossen's peers considered him a nasty piece of work. This always helped. But also, his own life and that of Tatyana depended on his success.

So now, Harry's immediate problem was to get close to Fossen, and this was aggravated by the need for some quick success. Rubeliev wanted Fossen dead before the succession meetings began, just as was required by his original contract. In Moscow, he had taken some time to make his preparations but not now, not today. Immediate action was required, and Harry swiftly decided on a full frontal attack.

He could think of no reason why he should not call Fossen and arrange a meeting to report his progress with their original contract. He had seen Fossen at the funeral and, although he had tried to keep a low profile, he thought it was quite probable that Fossen had also spotted him, hopefully believing that he was still in pursuit of Rubeliev. Embarrassingly, Rubeliev had run into him at the reception. Harry had cut the meeting very short and was fairly certain that Fossen had already left by then.

Way back in Naples, along with the dossier on Rubeliev, Fossen had given Harry his direct telephone number, and he dialled it now.

"Fossen," was the simple, sharp answer.

"Hey, Carl. Harry Fletcher here." He had decided to make Fossen as comfortable as possible by keeping the conversation on a friendly footing. "I saw you at the funeral, but we didn't get a chance to talk. I flew in from England to put Giovanni in the picture about our contract - my efforts to date. He invited me to Rico's funeral."

He lowered his voice to a conspiratorial level. "I was surprised to see the Russian, Rubeliev, there too. I thought at first it might present a new opportunity for me, but Giovanni insisted it shouldn't happen here - on home ground."

Harry paused for a moment before continuing, "Anyway, I did make my report to Giovanni, and he thought I ought to fill you in as well, so I said I'd call in here before I go back to Moscow. I'm staying at the New York-New York hotel. I wonder if you'd mind coming over here, and I'll bring you up to date."

"I'm very busy, Fletcher," Fossen replied more formally. "Could you come to my apartment please?"

This was the last thing Harry wanted, but he had prepared for it.

"Look, Carl. I've had an accident. I've damaged my arm and one of my legs. I don't think anything's broken, but my arm is in a sling, and my leg hurts to walk. And I don't know my way around this town. I'd much rather you'd come here if you wouldn't mind."

There was silence for a few seconds before Fossen spoke again. "OK. Where are you?"

"Room 7245 - it's on the seventh floor. I've got a couple of things I've got to do, so can we say – four o'clock this afternoon?"

"Very well," Fossen accepted. "I'll be there."

Harry did indeed have some preparations to do, but for the moment he felt hungry. He decided that, if all went well, he would be treating himself to a celebration dinner tonight, so he went downstairs for a quick beer and a sandwich.

When he had finished, he headed for the bell desk and was given directions to the nearest drugstore, where he purchased a proprietary arm sling and a box of painkillers.

Next, he made a methodical tour of the Casino and Shopping Mall floors of the hotel, working out and memorising a variety of routes to the various banks of staircases and elevators.

He then went in search of a suitable member of staff to assist him in a contingency plan that he had been working up in his mind. He guessed that the place would be stuffed with Fossen's men and was anxious to find someone who was not in his pay. Beside the bell desk, he spotted a possible candidate and started chatting to him. The fresh-faced young man introduced himself as Tom and said he was a student working his way through university. Ideal, thought Harry. A good offer to top up his beer fund produced a positive response to Harry's request for help, and this was endorsed by a nod from his Supervisor.

Harry escorted Tom to his room and explained in detail what he wanted from him. It was to be a surprise for a friend, and would only work if the timetable was followed to the letter. He then went over the whole operation a second time and jotted the timings down on a sheet of hotel notepaper. The lad assured him there would be no problem. Harry felt he could be trusted, paid him well and gave him a "don't let me down" pat on the back as he left.

He then set about positioning his weapons. He slid the Smith & Wesson into his trouser pocket. It was much too hot to wear a holster and a jacket to hide the gun, but he intended it as something of a loss leader. Anyone with Fossen's experience would be sure to spot it, but he would also surely expect a man in Harry's line of business to carry a gun anyway.

Similar experiences in the past led Harry to approach the coming meeting as a piece of theatre. The script would need to be largely improvised as the plot twisted in any variety of directions, and he would need to be prepared for any number of possible scenarios. Thorough preparation could give him the edge, however, and his next task was to dress the set very carefully.

Even if Fossen did not spot the Smith & Wesson in his pocket, he would be highly unlikely to use it. It would make far too much noise in a hotel environment. But he had to think carefully about positioning the Beretta with the silencer. "Noise suppressor" was a far more accurate term than a silencer. Harry was well aware that any shot from the gun would be anything but silent. He decided to secrete it in the bathroom. He should be able to improvise an excuse to visit it, either to use the toilet or to get some painkillers for his wounds.

Many years earlier, before their deployment in Iraq, both Harry and Bob had separately attended commando courses which had involved instruction in various methods of killing, both with and without hardware. As well as several types of firearms, it had included knives, smothering devices and many others. Years later, when Harry had come to sort out what Bob called his "bye-bye box", he had come across one of Bob's favourite assassination weapons. It was a ligature, given to him by a rich Sicilian industrialist for whom he had just completed a job. Beautifully constructed from plaited strands of fine flexible steel and with carved wooden handles at both ends, it was still small enough to be secreted in several ways. It was not one of Harry's favourite tools but, on a whim, he had brought it over to the States sewn into the collar of a windcheater he had packed, and he now placed it in one of the sideboard drawers, underneath Fossen's original dossier on Rubeliev. He should be able to find some excuse to refer to it during the meeting.

Harry looked at his watch and realised that Fossen must be on his way. He quickly tucked the knife in beside the ligature and shut the drawer. He stood still for a moment and surveyed the room. All seemed set.

Suddenly, he remembered his accident. He had not invented this excuse simply to persuade Fossen that he should visit him at his hotel. He knew well that, in any such meeting, it was important to put the victim as far as possible at his ease. Giving him an apparent physical advantage helped to do just that. In addition, the sling could provide a useful hiding place for whichever weapon he might decide to use. And finally, the sudden use of a limb thought to be damaged would add considerable surprise. These were all small advantages, but worth the preparation time.

He realised that there was not too much of this left now, and he ran into the bathroom tearing into the packaging to remove the sling. Placing it around his neck, he found it needed some adjustment and he had only partially finished this when, at almost precisely 4.00 pm, there was a knock at the door.

Chapter 21

Harry quickly finished adjusting the sling and slowly opened the door a few inches. Fossen stood there, unsmiling as usual, dapper in a formal suit and tie. "Fletcher," he said simply.

Harry swung the door open fully to let him in. As he did so, two burly men, one from behind each side of the door, emerged and pushed past Fossen. Both moved swiftly to demobilise Harry, locking his good arm behind his back. "Hey," he shouted out. "What the fuck's going on? Fossen, get your men off me. We're here to talk."

"We'll talk," Fossen said calmly, moving into the room and shutting the door behind him. "But I need to check you out first. It'll be much easier if you don't struggle. Just let my men search you."

"That's not friendly, Fossen," Harry said. But as the two heavies loosened their grip, he held up a hand in acceptance and let them frisk him, remembering to wince visibly as they checked his right arm. They found the Smith & Wesson immediately, of course, and after a further very thorough search they nodded to Fossen.

"OK," said Fossen. He took the gun from his men. "I'll take charge of this, Fletcher. If we're just here to talk, why were you carrying it?"

Harry shrugged. "I always carry it. It's part of me."

Fossen was silent for a few moments but then, seeming to accept the explanation, he said, "OK,

Fletcher. My reports tell me you haven't got far with our contract. But tell me about it."

Harry recounted the story just as he had reported it to Giovanni. When it came to the incident in the French restaurant, Fossen quizzed him closely about their escape. Harry had not had to describe this before and felt himself beginning to struggle. He started with them jumping onto a train without being caught. Eventually, his wife's good knowledge of the Russian Metro system had allowed them to make the right changes to reach the Paveletsky railway station, and from there to the airport where they were lucky to get an early flight to London.

Fossen stopped him there and said, "I think it might surprise you to learn, Fletcher, that I have more than one report that you were caught in the Metro station and taken away by Rubeliev and his men."

"That's nonsense," countered Harry immediately. "How would I be here now?" An obvious response, but things were starting to unravel quickly.

"That's precisely what worries me, Fletcher. Our sources are very sure of the facts. And if you were in the hands of Rubeliev, how indeed are you here? And what are you here for?"

Harry shook his head. "I'm sorry, Carl. I don't understand. Your sources are just plain wrong."

After a moment's thought, Fossen continued with another question. "How well do you know Rubeliev?"

"What! How do you mean 'know'?" I don't know him at all."

"But you have met him?"

"No! Of course not. I've seen him many times. I've even had him in my gun sights. But I wouldn't call that meeting him."

"So, if you passed him in the street, you wouldn't stop to shake his hand?"

Harry began to smell a trap. Had Fossen seen him with Rubeliev at the funeral reception? If so, he was in deep trouble. He was thankful now that he had set up a contingency rescue plan. He winced in pain and held his right hand. This allowed him to look at his watch surreptitiously. There were still several minutes before his plan was due to kick in.

"Of course not, Carl," he said, and then added, "Look. Your men were rough with my arm, and it's beginning to hurt badly. Do you mind if I get some painkillers from the bathroom?"

"I fear you're going to need more than painkillers where I am taking you, Fletcher. Your answers stink. You shook hands and held a conversation with Rubeliev at Rico's funeral wake, and I have my own eyes as witness to that."

Harry could think of nothing to say, as Fossen continued, "The question is, what does this all mean?" He paused and then continued, "I'm not sure. But I intend to find out, Fletcher, even if it kills you for me to do so. But this is not the right place. We're going to take you for a ride - to somewhere quieter, out in the country. A place you've already visited today."

Fossen stood there, thinking how they were to get a struggling man out to their car. Then, surprisingly, he looked at Harry and asked, "Where are your painkillers?"

"They're in the bathroom. I'll get them."

Harry tried to move but was held firmly by one of the heavies. Fossen looked at the other one and nodded in the direction of the bathroom. He left the room and was gone some little time, but when he returned he held up a pack of aspirins. Then, in his other hand, he held up the silenced Berretta.

He handed it to Fossen who looked at Harry, shaking his head. "I might have guessed," he said. "But that just settles the matter, doesn't it?

A moment later, all heads turned as there was a knock at the door and a call of "Room service".

Before Fossen could say anything, Harry called at the closed door, "Right. I'll be with you in a second."

Then, to Fossen, he explained, "I ordered a drinks trolley. I thought we could do with something..."

"Get rid of him," Fossen interrupted abruptly. "Tell him there's been a change of plan."

"OK. But I'll have to sign a chit," said Harry, and tried to move to the door. Fossen was wavering. "He won't go until I do," he added.

Fossen pulled out a revolver and hid it behind his back. "Just get rid of him, and don't even think of trying anything," he said sternly. He nodded to his men to release their grip.

Harry strode to the door and opened it wide. As good as his word, Tom was ready for him and immediately began to push the trolley of drinks into the doorway. Being a large hotel door, it was wide enough for Harry to swiftly slide alongside the trolley and out into the corridor. As soon as he was out, Tom feigned confusion and turned the trolley wedging it in the doorway and pushing it further into the room. Fossen and his men floundered furiously as they tried to follow Harry out.

Harry had always been a good sprinter, and he used the few precious seconds gained by running literally for his life down the long corridor, ripping off the sling and throwing it into the open doorway of a room that was being serviced. He reached the lobby and dived into the open elevator, quickly turned the key that Tom had used to lock it open on the seventh floor, and pressed the button for the Casino floor. The doors started closing agonisingly slowly, but they were already a narrow slit by the time Harry caught sight of Fossen turning into the lobby.

Whether his pursuers waited for another elevator or took to the stairs, Harry guessed that he had gained the best part of a minute as he exited the elevator and began walking briskly across the Casino floor, hoping to get lost in the noise and crowd of the gaming room.

But he was now in Fossen's home territory and in no time he spotted security staff with cell phones at their ears, scanning the floor with darting eyes. When he was only halfway across, Harry saw one of them appear to lock his eyes onto him and then immediately start moving towards him. Swiftly, Harry changed direction and started running away from his practised route. He came to an open service area and, with no time to wait for an elevator, he sprang onto the stairs which he took two at a time up to the second floor. He started to run in the direction that he judged would lead out onto The Strip.

Harry soon found himself running past a crowd of people who were standing and chattering against the building's external wall. He soon realised that he had stumbled across the line for the hotel's Big Apple roller coaster. Most of them looked glumly at him as he ran past them, and he heard mutterings and shouts of "Get back" and "Get in line."

Very soon, the queue gave way to a barrier with a notice which read "*Maintenance in progress. Please wait.*" There was no visible way out now except backwards towards a waiting Fossen so, placing one hand on the barrier, he hurdled it and started running up the platform. Maintenance engineers, who were doing some testing of equipment, looked around and started shouting at him to get back, but he was now committed. A four-car train was moving off as he barged past them. Just as the platform was running out, he managed to throw himself into the last compartment of the last car. Immediately a large padded security bar closed down on him, forcing him back into the seat.

The cars were moving along a track towards the outside of the hotel, but at a desperately slow rate. None of the engineers attempted to follow, however, remaining rooted to the spot where they stood, some on the platform and others on the track, with their arms folded staring at the outgoing train.

Harry's mind was racing. What would Fossen do when he caught up? Would he follow him, perhaps in the next car? Or would he simply wait for Harry to complete the circuit and return to the station?

As this last thought struck him, he realised that he would have to get off somewhere. He had never been on this ride before, but he was sure that he would not be able to get off it once it picked up speed, so he would have to do so before the cars started their first big drop. Just as he realised this the ride engaged with the rack and pinion mechanism which would power it to its very highest point.

Kerack Kerack Kerack Kerack Harry had to act quickly. He tried to lift the security bar but to no avail. It was stuck fast against his waist. He tried to drag his body up through the gap, but again it proved impossible. His legs would not bend the way they would have to. He was trapped underneath it.

Kerack Kerack Kerack If he was to get out, he would have to slide underneath the bar and somehow break open the door. He kicked at the left-hand door, but it failed to budge. It looked pretty heavy.

Kerack Kerack Kerack The car was now leaning backwards at around forty-five degrees and, turning his head, Harry caught sight of Fossen as he appeared round the end of the building and started to clamber along the wooden platform that ran either side of the track to the summit. He appeared to be alone, at least for the moment.

Kerack Kerack Kerack Harry managed to slide under the security bar and stretched his body out face down on the floor. He kicked back hard with one leg at the door, but nothing seemed to move. He would have to get more leverage somehow.

Kerack Kerack Kerack He managed to turn his body over so that he was now lying on his back, and could place his shoulder against the right-hand side of the car. He pulled both legs up as far as they would go before his knees hit the security bar and smashed them down onto the left-hand door. Nothing gave.

Kerack Kerack Kerack He did the same thing again, and once more there was no movement. Panic was beginning to set in. He wondered how much more of the climb there was. At any moment, the train would reach the summit and the cars would crash down the first and biggest incline – almost vertically. Would he survive this or the subsequent turns and upside-down loops?

Kerack Kerack Kerack It surely cannot be long now, as Harry put all his strength into another double leg kick. As he did so, whilst there was no apparent give in the door opposite, he felt a big movement in the door that was behind his back.

Kerack Kerack Kerack One more mighty push with both legs and the door behind him swung open.

Kerack Kerack Harry wriggled his body out onto the wooden walkway. With his back sliding along it, he managed to briefly grab hold of the side railings and pull the rest of his body and legs from the car.

Kerack... At the last moment, Harry's left leg must have caught on some metal on the car or the track, and he cried out in pain. But he was out.

WWRRRrrrrrr Harry watched the cars disappear with a roar over the top of the summit just a few feet from where he lay.

He pulled himself upright with the aid of the handrail and gingerly tested his leg. He could put his weight on it, but very painfully. At least it was probably not broken then, he thought.

But where was Fossen? Had he seen him escape from the car?

The question was answered immediately. Harry heard a loud *bang* and almost simultaneously a metallic *clang* followed by a *weeeee* as the bullet shot off the handrail at an angle. He instinctively pulled his hand quickly off the rail as he felt the impact.

Looking down the track, Harry could see Fossen about halfway up the walkway. He ducked as Fossen stopped and took aim once more, *bang clang weeeee...*

Harry had to move, and fast. He had already spotted a service ladder leading down from the summit. He limped to the top as rapidly as his leg would allow and somehow managed to throw it over the handrail onto the ladder. He heaved the rest of his body over and started to descend. He was able to make fast progress, sometimes slipping down several rungs at once.

After descending for around half a minute, he came across a steel gangway that ran horizontally through one of the loops in the ride. He felt it might make him a more difficult target for Fossen, who must be almost directly above him now. He left the ladder and started along it. After about forty yards or so, it led back onto the track later in its run at the foot one of the secondary long drops. Harry stepped back onto the trackside walkway, which was somewhat narrower here. He was still on the right-hand side of the track - the side he had left it, but now he had to cross over it to reach the next section of ladder leading down.

As he stepped onto the track, he heard a roar from his left. He had been so intently occupied, he had not noticed that the train was continuing to trundle round on a second lap of the track, and was at this very moment bearing down towards him, picking up speed down the slope. Quickly, he leapt onto the left-hand walkway, turned around and flattened the back of his body against the guardrails.

The cars must have passed with at least a foot to spare, but the speed and the noise at that proximity were terrifying. After the last one had disappeared around the next sharp bend, it was a second or two before Harry could get his head together. But he was acutely aware that Fossen was closing behind him as he staggered onto the ladder. After only a short drop, it led onto a further walkway that ran back again underneath the track.

He had managed to limp some thirty feet along this when he came up against a control panel, with a couple of dials and an array of switches. But the gangway itself just ended. Panic began to rise once more as Harry desperately peered over each side in turn. No ladders. Nothing. He was at a dead end.

He began to look further afield. There was a new ladder leading straight down, but it was attached to a separate section of track and was about twelve feet away. The only way to get there would be to hang from a steel cross beam. On a good day, Harry might have felt able to take it on, but not in his current state, and he turned to retrace his steps.

But as he did so, he heard Fossen above him. He only had to reach the track and Harry would be completely exposed – a sitting duck. Desperately, he looked back at the ladder, wondering if he could reach it after all. But it was all too late as he saw Fossen step onto the trackside, turn and look straight down on him from only about twenty feet away.

Harry stood there, quite still, caught like a rabbit in the headlights. For the very first time, he saw Fossen truly smile. But it held no humour. Pleasure, yes, but no humour. And in no time, it morphed into a sarcastic, sneering grin as he slowly raised his gun. Time stood still for Harry as images flashed through his mind, like a speeded-up screen saver of family photos - but most of all, of Tatyana.

Harry dropped to his knees at the very moment that Fossen squeezed the trigger. He yelled out in agony as his damaged leg hit the steel. The bullet hit the handrail and ricocheted off. He moved to the right as Fossen took aim once more.

But before he was able to fire, Harry saw Fossen's head whip round to his right and at the same time heard the roar of the train as it again started down the slope. Fossen briefly dropped his gun hand and, still staring down at Harry, forced the front of his body into the guardrails. As with Harry, the cars passed by comfortably behind him, still gaining speed. Harry had nowhere to run, Fossen simply kept him in his gaze, still smiling, and then slowly raised his gun for the final kill.

As the last car passed, the heavy door that Harry had forced open, and which had been flapping wildly all the way round, slammed into Fossen. All of the air, and probably most of the life, were instantly forced out of him. His body was lifted four, five, six feet into the air, over the handrail and it started to spin directly down towards Harry.

Now standing up, he saw Fossen's head catch the steel gangway floor just a few feet away. It snapped back with a sickening *crack*, and his whole body continued spiralling downwards. He stood motionless, listening to a bizarre symphony of sound – the noise of the train fading as it continued along its tortuous path, Fossen's gun clattering onto the metal walkways, police sirens wailing as they began to arrive in droves, Fossen's body as it thumped into sections of steelwork, and the final *crump* as his body hit the ground below and lay spread-eagled on the terrazzo floor.

Harry looked down. There was blood all over the gangway beneath his feet, dripping through the grill, and was still pumping from his leg. He was beginning to feel faint and knew he must act quickly. The Gods had spared him this day and he owed it to them to survive somehow.

He made his way back under the track. Painfully, he lifted his damaged leg onto the ladder and started down once more. It took him almost five minutes to negotiate the series of walkways and ladders. As he stepped off the final rung, he was circled by half a dozen cops with guns drawn and trained on him, screaming at the tops of their voices for him to, "Get down. Down on the floor". Very faint now, Harry flopped painfully onto the ground and lay there spread-eagled, a mirror image of Fossen just a few feet away.

He felt himself being carefully frisked for the third time that day, until a voice shouted, "He's clean". Hands grabbed him beneath the shoulders and he felt himself being dragged along the ground and then bundled unceremoniously into the back seat of a car. He heard a brief single wail of a siren and the car moving off.

Then the deep blackness descended once more.

Chapter 22

Beep...Beep...Beep...Beep...

The sound arrived slowly into Harry's consciousness. He recognised it, but couldn't place it. What was it, and where had he heard it before? He could not remember, but he wasn't concerned. He was far too weary and dropped once more into unconsciousness.

Beep...Beep...Beep...Beep...

There it was again. Harry recognised it this time. He tried to open his eyes. As he did so, he heard a female voice saying, "Mr Fletcher," then again, "Mr Fletcher". Gradually, a black face came out of the fog. It was a pretty black face. It was a pretty and smiling black face that spoke again, "Mr Fletcher. You're in hospital. You're going to be fine." He smiled slightly and slipped back into unconsciousness.

Beep...Beep...Beep...Beep...

Harry opened his eyes again. Now he knew what it was, and where he was. He soon tired of staring at the ceiling and turned his head to look around the room. A nurse, who was shuffling some instruments on a tray, turned and saw that he was awake. She went to a telephone on the wall and spoke into it softly, then came over to the bed saying cheerily, "Good morning, Mr Fletcher."

Harry licked his dry lips and said simply, "Morning nurse."

She continued, "the doctor will be with you shortly. Can I get you anything? Is there anything you'd like to know?"

"What time is it?" he croaked.

She looked at her watch, "Nearly eleven thirty." As she was saying this, she turned as the door opened and a man in a white tunic entered, along with another nurse. The man stepped up to Harry's bedside.

"Good morning Mr Fletcher. My name's Jack Moore. You were brought in yesterday afternoon with a nasty cut on your leg. It was pretty deep, I'm afraid, and you'd lost an awful lot of blood." He sounded very matter-of-fact as he continued, "Well. We've topped that up and stitched the leg. Nothing was broken, so you'll be fine in no time. Just take it easy for a day or two. OK?"

"Thanks, Doc," Harry said weakly.

"How are feeling? There are a couple of detectives outside wanna have a word with you. Do you feel up to it – if I say they can have a couple of minutes only?"

"Yes," Harry agreed. "So long as they don't stay too long. I feel so sleepy."

The doctor strode quickly to the door. As he opened it, Harry noticed a uniformed cop in the corridor outside. The doctor and nurse left and, after a few words outside, were replaced by two detectives in plain clothes. Harry had only a couple of moments to work up his story as the two men approached, flashing their LVPD identity cards.

"Hi. I'm DI Haggerty, and this here's Sergeant March." The lead detective was a tall gaunt man with an angular face and a sharp nose. He bent, almost reverentially, down to Harry.

"I hear you won't be released 'till tomorrow," he said, and then promised, "We'll talk some more then. But I do have a couple of questions I'd like some answers to right now if you don't mind." He sat down on a chair by the bed, with his sergeant remaining standing behind him.

Harry gave him a silent nod and Haggerty continued, "Did you know the man who was chasing you?"

"No," Harry began. "I really can't think what it was all about..."

"How did it start?"

Harry shook his head. "We were in the shopping mall under my hotel. I'm just an English tourist..."

He was finding it difficult to concentrate, trying to find a reasonable explanation. "...it was crowded, and I bumped into this guy. He went mad and punched me. I'm afraid I reacted and hit him back. He had friends with him, and they all started on me. I just ran. And he had a gun..."

Harry paused then, catching his breath. The detective said nothing but looked at him quizzically. He continued, "I managed to get away by leaping into a lift, but they all followed up the stairs. I came to a dead end on the rollercoaster and jumped into a car that was leaving. Next thing I knew that man was chasing and firing a gun at me. Some people! They get so angry at the slightest thing. I just don't understand it..."

The detective was silent again, but Harry said no more. Eventually, Haggerty rose from his chair and said, "OK, Mr Fletcher. That'll be all for now. There'll be an officer outside your door all night – for your protection. When they release you from here, he'll bring you to the station for a few more questions. You get some rest now."

As he went out of the door, he turned back briefly and said, "Oh. I've got your passport. I'm keeping it for the moment." With that, he turned to speak briefly to the uniformed officer and then left.

Midway through the following morning, Harry was released from the hospital with a walking stick, some painkillers and advice to take things easy for the next few days. Strangely, he thought, there were no hassles about medical fees or expenses, but he was so very tired and let it ride.

Whether or not they believed his story at the police station, Harry will never know. But the additional questioning turned out to be a rudimentary and half-hearted affair. The body had quickly been identified as Carl Fossen, and they were more than happy to learn of one fewer villain on their patch – "a very nasty piece of work" was how Haggerty described him to Harry.

After only a couple of hours, he shook hands with DI Haggerty as he returned his passport.

"I don't know quite who you are, Mr Fletcher. And I do believe there's more to all this than you're telling me. But I can't think of anything sensible to charge you with, so off you go."

Then, after a short pause, he added, "But I want you out of the country. Right now. I can't be responsible for your safety outside this building. I'll hand you over to Sergeant Hammer. He'll set you on your way."

"Bye," Harry said simply. "Thanks." He was perfectly happy to be hustled out of the country. He was free of his ordeal and a warm feeling of euphoria was beginning to set in.

Chapter 23

A quarter of an hour later, Harry's elation had evaporated as the cab bumped along the dirt track towards McCauley's Rest. He had been hijacked, presumably by the Mob. Somewhere along the line, he had been betrayed by someone in their pay. He almost shouted out in anger – the Desk Sergeant. Sergeant Bloody Hammer!

The journey was agony for Harry. He was mentally shattered. With all his hopes of a soft landing now gone, his mindset had been thrown into sudden reverse, and he could only conceive of the fate that would surely soon await him. His body too was suffering painfully, with his injured leg jarred by every jolt as the cab lurched at each gulley and knoll. It was almost a relief when it reached its destination and pulled up sharply beside a large black four-wheel drive vehicle.

Three men who Harry did not recognise emerged from the front door of the diner, each holding a revolver, and surrounded the cab. Harry heard a loud *click* as the driver released the rear door locks, but he remained seated. One of the men moved to the cab and pulled open the door beside him. Without uttering a word, he ordered him out with a sweep of his gun hand.

As they entered the diner, a fourth man rose from one of the chairs ranged along the side of the room and approached Harry.

"We haven't met," he began easily, with an accent that suggested an English origin. "My name's Will Brolin."

Like all the others in the room, he was a big man, probably younger than he looked, for he had a shaved head. He might well have been good-looking, but for a large strawberry birthmark that ran up his right neck and covered most of his right cheek.

"Now!" he began simply, "Why did you kill my boss - Carl Fossen?"

Harry did not know how to answer and was silent for a moment or two. For want of something better, he decided to give out the same story as he had given to the police. This proved to be a big mistake. The cab driver had now joined them and, when Brolin looked at him for confirmation, he shook his head. Harry had forgotten that the man had been at his meeting with Fossen and knew the whole sequence of events.

"I think not," said Brolin, and paused briefly. "Carl didn't confide in me with his reasons, but I know that he had become fearful for his safety over recent days. For a start, he put out an alert if you ever showed your face in Vegas. You were identified a couple of times, once in the New York-New York hotel and later out here. What the fuck were you doing out here anyway?"

Harry did not answer.

"Well, that doesn't matter now. But your reason for wanting Carl dead does interest me, and I intend to find out before you die."

"Yes, you have my word on it. You will not be leaving this place alive this afternoon. Carl may have been no angel, but I owe that to him at least. My problem is only the manner of your death. How would Carl have arranged it, I ask myself?"

Harry winced internally at the thought, but he was already resigned to his likely fate and said nothing. With an air of defiance, he took a chair to the centre of the room and sat down saying, "My leg hurts. I hope you don't mind."

If his action was intended to anger Brolin, it failed miserably. He smiled, picked up a length of cord and threw it to one of his men, ordering him to tie Harry to the chair. His hands were secured behind the chair's back, and he grimaced as his injured leg was bound firmly to the front chair leg. Over the last few days, Harry had looked death in the face on more than one occasion but now, helpless and surrounded by men bent on vengeance, he felt that the end was closer and more certain than ever.

As Brolin approached Harry, his face no longer showed any trace of a smile, and he asked in a low, measured voice, full of menace, "So, Fletcher. We reach the sharp end. I will ask you once again. Why did you wish to kill Carl Fossen?"

Harry said nothing and stared steadily back into Brolin's eyes. But almost inevitably his eyes were drawn down to the violent red patch of skin on his face. It may have been this movement of his eye to Brolin's deformity or it may simply have been his silence, but Brolin suddenly leant back and punched him hard on his left cheek.

Harry did not immediately lose consciousness but the whole of the left side of his face was ablaze with pain, and he felt dizzy. He looked up to see Brolin holding and rubbing his hand.

"You hurt my hand, you bastard," he growled.

Brolin had tired of any personal involvement and nodded to the burliest of his men to continue the interrogation. The man returned his gun to its secreted holster and, with a smirk of relish, took off his jacket and moved towards Harry. As he did so, he stopped suddenly and reached once again for his gun.

The heads of everyone in the room turned at the sound of a car screeching to a halt right outside the front door. They all trained their weapons on the door, silently waiting for it to open. After just a few seconds, another two large men entered. They held no weapons in their hands but shot them up into the air as they caught sight of all the guns facing them.

"Who the fuck are you?" demanded Brolin.

At that moment, against the brilliant desert sun outside, an even bulkier silhouette filled the doorway. But only as the man stepped forward did his features become visible. "They're with me", he said softly.

Brolin's jaw dropped visibly, but he managed to shout out, "Giovanni!"

Harry could hardly believe his eyes. Had the cavalry arrived in time? Was this one final chance of salvation, or had Giovanni arrived merely to witness the execution?

These questions were answered almost immediately as Giovanni said gently, "You're making a mistake, Will." He waited for some reaction from this odd circle of men as they stood with mouths open and their guns still trained on him, wondering what the hell was going on.

Brolin eventually broke the silence. "This man killed Carl," he insisted.

Giovanni shook his head. "It was an accident, Will," he said quietly.

Will's father had been a friend of Giovanni and had run one of the more successful gangs in England, but he had been arrested and sent down for a considerable stretch. Will's mother had died some years earlier and, concerned about his son's future, he had contacted Giovanni from prison and asked him if he would take care of him in America. Giovanni had agreed, and eventually, Will had become one of his most successful acolytes. His calm efficiency under pressure had stood him out from the crowd, and Giovanni had taken him personally under his wing. Brolin had worked for him for years until eventually, wanting to gain more experience, he had joined Fossen as his second in command in Las Vegas. Over the years, Giovanni had instilled in him the rules and customs of the Mafia, and he realised now the difficulty he would face in dissuading the man from what he perceived to be his sacred duty.

After a brief pause, Giovanni continued, "We've known each other a long time, Will. D'you trust me?"

"Sure! I trust you, Giovanni. You know I do," Brolin insisted. "And you know I'll be voting for you next week - or whenever it is."

Harry grinned. "I'm afraid you won't, Will. By tomorrow morning my name will be off the list."

Once again, Brolin's jaw dropped and his face became a picture of confusion. "You can't mean that," he protested. "We need you."

Giovanni's grin was gone now as he said, "I'm sorry, Will. But that's the way it is."

After a brief pause for thought, Giovanni turned to the men around him and said, "You can all stow your pieces, boys. This guy ain't no threat to any of us."

They looked nervously at their boss, but slowly began to put away their guns as Giovanni moved over to Harry. "You OK Harry?" he asked.

With his left jaw now bulging visibly, Harry didn't reply but simply nodded. Giovanni gave him a brief pat on the back and then moved back towards Will Brolin.

"Listen, you guys," he started, speaking to the room in general, "Will here and I have to talk. Lose yerselves outside for a while. We'll call yer when we're through."

As Giovanni's two men started for the door, the others looked once more at Brolin for confirmation. He paused for only a brief moment before giving them a nod.

"It's all a horrible fucking mess, Will" Giovanni began when the three were alone, "and Fletcher here is part of it. It ain't his fault. He just got caught up in it, and much of it is down to me."

Brolin clearly did not understand. "You say it was an accident. Maybe it did end accidentally, but Fletcher was out to kill Carl. I know neither of us liked the man, but we do have to avenge him. It's part of our code."

"I know, Will. I know. But codes and rules, they're all made to be broken on occasion. I've had to bend them more than once myself. And anyway, it's not clear to me who was out to kill who. I know Fossen arrived at a meeting they'd arranged with loads of muscle. And I also know that Fletcher was unarmed when he was chased onto the coaster..."

"But it was our man who got killed," Brolin interrupted.

"Yup." Giovanni paused briefly, and then continued, "Let me give you some of the background. It's real complicated, but I'll try to make it brief."

"I was never going to put my name forward for Rico's job. I'm too old, Will. And I don't have the energy that's needed - not now. I told Rico this and we discussed other options. Neither of us fancied the idea of Joe Becker in Chicago, and it was Rico who came up with the name of the Ruskie. I would have wished for a Yank, of course, but I've met Rubeliev – and he's good. We just have to work with what we've got, eh? Anyways, in the end, we both agreed to support him."

"Then your man, Carl Fossen, turned up." He sighed heavily. "He knew he'd never get the job himself, so he set himself up as some sort of king-maker. He decided my name might get me the job, and he came to see me. I told him I wasn't interested."

"And then he blackmailed me."

"I'm not going into any detail on that, Will. Just to say it was something to do with the family – some old history. He was a real bugger. He'd got files stashed away to blackmail pretty well everyone with any influence. He probably had one on you too, Will."

"Anyway, like an idiot, I fell for it. I agreed to stand, knowing full well that if I did get the job he would be pulling my strings forever."

"But the Russian was still out in front, all the time gathering momentum, and that didn't suit his plan. So he came up with this crackpot scheme to have him assassinated. He wanted to do it himself, for Chris' sake. I managed to dissuade him from that, but he was adamant, and insisted it should be done."

Brolin listened patiently as Giovanni continued, "Remember, Will, it was Rico's choice of successor that I was expected to have killed! I was boxed in – and very unhappy."

"Then I hit on a plan. I would set up a contract with someone unsuitable – someone who was doomed to fail in the job. There's one or two I'm sure we can both think of, but we clearly couldn't use one of our own – much too dangerous if it ever came to light."

"Then I remembered this Englishman, this ... well, this amateur. I was sure he'd never get anywhere near a hit like Rubeliev, and I'm ashamed to say that I set him up - a patsy." He looked over at the sad figure slumped in the chair and said, "I'm sorry, Harry. You didn't deserve it, but I was desperate. And if it's any consolation, you got far nearer than I ever expected. I was getting real worried - thought I might have to warn Rubeliev at one stage."

"Anyway," he turned to Brolin, "I talked up his credentials and managed to convince Fossen that he was our man. We met with him, and a big fat fee persuaded him to take on the contract. He didn't succeed of course – at least, not in time."

"I don't know if it was this failure or something else entirely, but Fossen took a dislike to him, went to a meeting with him, disarmed him and threatened to kill him. But Harry managed to escape and was chased onto the hotel rollercoaster. The rest I think you know..."

Giovanni judged that Brolin was wavering and pushed on, "Trust me on this, Will. Fletcher has worked for us more than once. He's a friend of the outfit."

Brolin still looked unresolved and said nothing. Giovanni pushed one more time, "I know how you feel, Will. But I'm tellin' yer – it ain't no sign of weakness. It's a big man who can back down at the right time. And that's what I'm asking yer to do now. Please. Release Fletcher into my care. Whatcha say?"

Harry's ears were still ringing from Brolin's punch, but through the noise and pain, he had been listening intently to the ebb and flow of the conversation. Now he held his breath as Brolin continued to waiver.

The seconds seemed like minutes as Brolin wrestled with his conscience. Finally, he appeared to make up his mind. Harry's heart sank when he said nothing but reached into his pocket and, with a quick flick, a long steel blade emerged from a bone handle and he moved towards Harry.

Then, with deft hands, he sliced Harry's bindings.

"Thanks, Will," said Giovanni, as he went over to Brolin and shook his hand. "I do appreciate it. Yer did right, I promise you."

Harry stood up gingerly, rubbing his arms where they had been tied. As Giovanni approached him, there was no great show of emotion - no great bear hug, just another swift shake of hands as he led him out into the light.

It was still very hot outside, and the car was like an oven until the air conditioning began to kick in. Nevertheless, Harry was able to make himself reasonably comfortable wedged beside the mass that was his rescuer. He was alive, and it seemed now that he was finally on his way home.

They were silent for several minutes as Harry struggled to cushion the effects of the humps and gullies on his injured leg. It was he who finally broke the silence, "The cavalry arrived only just in time, Giovanni," said Harry.

Giovanni smiled wryly. "You're lucky it arrived at all. I heard you were being released and called at the Station to pick you up. Then I had a hell of a job getting the real story out of the Desk Sergeant."

"Listen, Harry. I'm not good at apologies. I just ain't used to 'em. And I sure ain't repeating today's. It just seemed the only way at the time. I hope you can see that."

Harry did not say anything, but looked round at Giovanni and smiled weakly. And that was it. Nothing more on the subject was ever said.

After another short silence, Giovanni continued, "You OK Harry? I heard you'd buggered your leg."

"It's not too bad thanks," he replied. "It hurts when I walk, but the Doc assures me I'll be back to normal in a couple of weeks."

Giovanni looked at Harry's face and ran his fingers down his left cheek saying, "They rough you up a bit in there, Harry?"

"Nothing too serious - thanks to you. They'd only just started when you turned up. I'm good, thanks."

"Good!"

Then Giovanni broke into a broad grin and said, "That was quite a show you gave us on the coaster, Harry."

Harry responded merely with another sheepish grin.

There was silence then until they reached the highway and were on the outskirts of Vegas, when Giovanni started again, "Now let me bring you up to date, Harry. As you heard in there, I'm taking my name out of the race to succeed Rico. It'll mean the Ruskie should get the job. I know Rico would have approved. And I guess it won't be so bad having a foreigner for a boss. My own family were foreigners once..."

"I've got a small bag of your things on the back seat. Christ, you travel light, Harry. I've settled all your bills - the hotel and the hospital. And I've got you a ticket to London - first class, Harry. Thought you might need to get some sleep. There's a plane just after five, and we're on our way to the airport right now."

"Thanks, Giovanni," said Harry. "That's good of you."

"That's the least I can do. I still owe you, Harry. And if there's anything more I can do for you - just ask. I mean that."

"I know, Giovanni. Thanks again."

They fell to silence again then. Both of them knew that this was probably the last time they would see each other, but neither wanted to admit or talk about it.

"Here we are." Giovanni perked up as the cab drew up at McCarran's departures set down area. He got out, retrieved a smart New York-New York plastic bag from the back seat and handed it to Harry along with the plane ticket. He opened his arms to him for one last hug. Then he said, "OK if I leave you here, buddy?"

"Sure, Giovanni. And you look after yourself, you great bear. Bye now."

"Ciao, Harry"

As he crossed through the entrance doors, Giovanni shouted after him, "And be sure to give my love to Tatyana". Harry raised his hand in acknowledgement without looking back, and disappeared from view.

The plane touched down in the early evening, and Harry took a taxi from Heathrow. As it pulled up outside the house, he got out and paid the driver, who drove off immediately. He stood for a while outside his gate, savouring the delicious anticipation of Tatyana shortly welcoming him home.

Then he opened the gate and limped swiftly up the short path to the door.

Printed in Great Britain
by Amazon